A Little Bit of Love...

To Digest A Spicy Life

A Little Bit of Love...

To Digest A Spicy Life

Tushar Taneja

Srishti
PUBLISHERS & DISTRIBUTORS

Srishti Publishers & Distributors
N-16, C. R. Park
New Delhi 110 019
editorial@srishtipublishers.com

First published by
Srishti Publishers & Distributors in 2011
4th impression 2015

All characters in this book are fictitious, and any resemblance to real persons, living or dead, is coincidental.

Printed and bound in India.

Dedicated to,

My Late Grandfather

With whom I spent countless wonderful Moments

Acknowledgement

The book in your hands is not just a book; it is a dream coming true. It is a dream I saw when I was studying in MNIT, Jaipur; A dream to become a writer. To make this dream come true, I had to sit home doing nothing but writing and thinking about this book for about one year but all that is history now. It would be very wrong if I don't give the persons their due respect for the efforts they made to make this dream a reality for without their help, this was perhaps impossible to make it happen.

Starting from the start, it was my friend 'Vishwanath' who prompted me to write this book and was with me all the way from the beginning. He was an unconditional help whenever I felt low. I would be thankful for the inspiration I got from my brother cum friend, Pravesh. Also the support I got from my parents is also something which kept me moving. I am lucky that I got such a great family.

I would like to thank the team of Srishti Publishers who worked very hard to make this book a success. I am really thankful for their continuous support and guidance through every step in publishing this book. Otherwise it was only the words I had; it is because of them that these words have now taken the shape of a book.

Finally I would thank to all the persons who came in my life and gave me the experiences which helped me to write this book. They taught me that life is not in branded clothes, expensive accessories or spending time at pubs with lot of wine. Life is in moments; moments filled with empathy, sympathy, trust and respect towards one's own relationships. In this book, I have tried to return this people what I got from them and I hope you will like my bit of love.

Prologue

For a family in which the head had died only a few days back, the environment in the house was not exactly what would have been elsewhere. Everybody in the house was trying certain maneuver to figure out the exact equation and make the most of the situation. And why this should not happen, when the owner of the house had left a property worth billions of rupees specifying no clear successor. People were making claims for the property but the person most likely to be the heir was feeling suffocated in this enigma and packing his luggage to leave as soon as possible. That gave a hard time to the person, who was trying to stop him.

"Why do you want to leave so early? I know you don't have anything important to do."

"What do you know about me? I have lots of things to do. I cannot afford to waste my time here anymore."

'Waste my time', how can he 'waste' his time here? This is his damn home.

"Your father just died and you cannot even wait for few months here till everything settles down. You have a big property to take care of. What kind of a son are you?"

"Don't give me that psychological crap. I know all you want is to win this property for me and have fame and money out of it."

Yes sir, I do want to have this high profile case in my kitty and with you, I have the best chance to win it.

"You are getting it all wrong. You know my father worked for yours all his life, now when he has retired, it is my duty to take care of you. Your father would have liked it, wouldn't he?"

"I don't know all that. First of all, uncle Ranjit is taking care of all this property so I don't have to bother. Second, I don't want to listen to people saying what my father would have liked. I don't have any interest in this property."

He is insane, even people who don't have any remote connection, have interest in this property. A small share can make them a millionaire.

"Listen, may be you don't have any interest in it, what if your uncle loses, or gets a very small share. With so many people hungry for this property there is a good chance that it will end up in safe hands if you also stake a claim. Plus you don't have to do anything. You just sign these papers and I will take care of the rest."

"Ok, tell me where to sign. I don't have time to let you try and convince me. I should better not argue with a lawyer." 'Prince' eventually surrendered in front of his lawyer's wish. *A prince by chance, not by choice.*

Finally, there was a sigh of relief as Mike opened his briefcase and handed over some papers and a pen telling him where to sign. Approval came sooner than he expected. He looked closely at the signatures which showed the name of the prince, A. Yashwardhan.

After all the papers were signed, 'Prince' asked,

"So who are the other people claiming this property?"

"Almost all your relatives; but they won't get any major share for sure. There are two important claims apart from yours; one is your uncle Ranjit's and second, a woman who claims to be your father's widow."

"Hmm, do you know anything about her?"

"She came out of the blue. Nobody in the family knows her. She may be genuine or just a whore trying her luck. I doubt whether she has any documents to prove her claim."

"That means I have the best chance of winning this property."

"Yes, and you are leaving. Anyways, where are you going?"

"That's none of your business." With a sharp reply 'Prince' slung his bag on his shoulder and started walking towards the door.

NEW APARTMENT

It was raining when the cab stopped with a jerk outside a high rise building. By this time Roshen was fast asleep. The driver woke him up. He pulled his luggage out of the cab and paid the driver. Squinting, he glanced towards the, Vrindawan Apartments. It looked like an old building from outside where the accommodation had been arranged by his friend because it was of course, least expensive and close to his new office.

"I have told your roommate that you would be coming tonight" Sangeet, Roshen's friend and colleague had told him on phone earlier that day.

"But I will reach there after midnight. Won't it be a problem?"

"Nah, you just reach there and join duty as soon as possible and remember, your apartment number is 507, 5th floor. Good night."

"OK, Good night" said Roshen but before he completed, the line was already cut and all he could hear was a beep.

He dragged his bag and got into the lift. There was no watchman around but this did not really bother him. There was very little in his luggage to worry about. No gadgets, no expensive belongings, just some cloths and books. *507, 5th floor, he reminded himself.*

Soon he was standing in front of his apartment and to his surprise; the door was wide open even at that time of the night. It was still raining outside but the open doors at this hour worried him a little. He switched on the torch in his cell phone which threw very small amount of light. With muddy feet, he entered the apartment for the first time in his life, without knowing that for the rest of his life, he will always remember it.

Across the hall, was the kitchen and space for dining but till now, the apartment looked completely empty except some papers and clothes on the floor. As Roshen moved a few steps ahead, he saw some light coming from a room which was across the hall. He knocked on the door but nobody responded. The door was not bolted so he slid the door open to see a person playing games on a laptop with his ears covered with headphones. This was the weirdest room he had ever seen in his life.

As Roshen opened the door, he was welcomed by the smell of cigarette smoke. The room was lit with a big yellow bulb. A very large painting replica of Mona Lisa was hanging on the wall in front of him but it was upside down. On the extreme right side of the room was a bed but instead of bed sheet, it was covered with a layer of books. On the table, there was an open CPU of a computer but no monitor or keyboard or anything else. A tennis racket, a cricket bat, one case of DVDs of 'FRIENDS' and few pen and pencils were also on the table but everything was covered with a layer of dust as it had not been touched for last few months. The floor was full of papers and in one corner of the room were some dirty clothes but that bunch still looked good compared to the rest of the room. The owner of the room was sitting on the floor with a pillow under him, smoking and playing some car racing game on his laptop with his back towards the door. As Roshen opened the door, his presence was felt and the owner removed his headphones and turned to him.

"Hi, you must be Roshen, I am Abhi. I was waiting for you. Do you want a drag?" he said offering Roshen a cigarette in a voice which was extra sophisticated but did not sound formal at all. He was bearded and had quite long hair.

"No thanks, sorry for making you wait. Can I have the keys to my room?"

"Don't say sorry, I am usually awake till this hour, so no big deal. Your keys are in the drawer. And if you want some water, it is there in the bottle. It is not very cold though. Make yourself comfortable. Tell me if you need something else. I will take you to the market tomorrow. We can do some shopping for you to settle down here." Abhi said all this in one breath all of which felt a little awkward to Roshen.

I have just met this guy and he is being extra friendly to me. I wonder why? But he did not say a word. Looked for his keys and lunged towards the door of the other room which was going to be his.

"Good night" he heard while leaving the room. He turned and said good night with a fake smile on his face. He just did not realize that it was the start of a lifelong friendship.

The next day was very busy for Roshen. Abhi woke him up at seven in the morning and got him tea and sandwiches. Abhi was surprisingly helpful about everything and Roshen, who was initially feeling very strange about his friendly behavior, soon got used to it and found it very comfortable being with him. Abhi took him to the market where they did not buy anything. They went instead to a cinema hall to watch a movie. The movie was a comedy flick 'The Hangover' and both laughed all the way. Then they went to a mall where Abhi did most of the shopping while Roshen was just following him. Abhi kept talking all the way. The only time Roshen experienced sense of emptiness was when Abhi started talking on his phone. Perhaps a girlfriend, he thought but didn't ask. He was having fun in this new city and with a good job; he expected a pleasant stay here.

The day was full of shopping, ice-creams, junk food and cigarettes. Roshen however did not smoke as much as Abhi, but he gave him company by taking some puffs. They did not take lunch. They did not even need it. By eight in the evening, when they decided to go back to their apartment, Abhi grabbed four bottles of beer for both of them.

"Let's go to your room, I am going to change. I will join you in few minutes." said Roshen, as he was a little reluctant to drink in his room. He did not certainly want his room to look like Abhi's.

"Make it fast." said Abhi disappearing in his room.

Roshen came back to his room and thought about the day. He had just met Abhi and he treated him like an old friend. Movie, shopping and now beer, his behavior made him wonder for a moment whether Abhi was gay, but he decided against it as the way he glanced to the girls he saw in the city today, *he must be straight*.

By the time Roshen came to Abhi's room, he had everything arranged for a drinking session. The room was lit by a red night lamp. Slow songs were being played on his laptop, a playlist which was probably prepared for such sessions, some snacks with two open bottles were there on the floor and on one side, Abhi was sitting, waiting for Roshen to join him.

"So Abhi, what exactly do you do?" said Roshen as he was thinking of something to start with.

"Nothing." Came a sharp reply. Probably Abhi was tired or he did not want to talk about what he really did. Then there was a silence for few minutes which made Roshen feel very awkward. Firstly, he was drinking beer for which he had not paid and secondly, he had known the person offering this beer for less than twenty-four hours and he was being suspiciously kind to him. But it took only half bottle for Abhi to speak and once he started, there was nothing stopping him.

"I am an engineer." He paused for a moment and started again.

"Unemployed engineer." he paused again. This reminded Roshen of James Bond and his style, *my name is Bond, James Bond.* But he remained silent as he knew Abhi had a lot more to say.

"I graduated from IIT Bombay three years back. Then I joined a construction company but I left the job in 2 months when I figured out that this is not what I want to do."

Roshen was both impressed and surprised.

"Daddy always wanted me to join our family business but I never had any interest in it. I stayed home for some time but it was difficult for both my family and me. So I took up a job and left home. I left that job within few days but never told anybody at home. They don't care about my job. I get fifty thousand bucks every month from my family, so you see; I don't even need a job."

"So you are living here and doing nothing for the last two years." said Roshen as he had just started feeling that he was sitting with a talented IIT graduate who was a bigger loser than he himself was.

"Not exactly, I have been writing short stories for a local magazine here. They are fond of love stories and I can write as many as I want. This is something I like to do, not because I have to do something." Said Abhi with his voice getting louder with each word, "and who says that doing something is necessary for life, when I can stay happy doing nothing. I don't believe in getting involved in the rat race to do something, get a job, then get married, have kids and spend the rest of your life bringing them up. I am happy this way and I will live my life this way only."

"Do you have girl friend?" asked Roshen as he desperately wanted to change the topic and what could have been a better topic than girls?

"Well, I had one." Said Abhi with a note of depression in his voice and took a large sip from his bottle, "we broke up about a year back."

"Oh, so now you don't have any."

"Now..." his tone suddenly changed, "I have many."

Roshen looked at him for a moment and they both burst into laughter.

1ST DAY IN OFFICE

The next day, Roshen woke up quite early in the morning with a different feeling. It was his first day in the new office and second in a new city. Abhi was still sleeping, his doors were wide open. Roshen thought about the instructions given by his parents before leaving home, don't trust strangers, take care of your stuff, have proper food properly and lot more. They were so many that he hardly remembered them but he realized that he had done exactly the opposite the very first day by having beer with a person he had known only for a few hours. *I can steal from Abhi's room. He has more valuable things than me and he is far more irresponsible about it, a fact that made him feel a little less guilty.*

Roshen wore a white shirt with small blue checks, a neatly ironed pair of black trousers and leather shoes for the office. He put some extra oil in his hair and combed it neatly. *Ready for the big day.* When he reached the office, he was as nervous as he had been at the time of the interview but this time more than ten minutes early.

The office was like an array of randomly placed cubicles and some small rooms consisting of two large conference rooms. Almost every employee had a computer and as the reporting time was approaching, every seat was being occupied. But Roshen had no idea whom to talk to. There was no one to attend to him and he felt helpless for a moment. But before he could think of going and talking to someone, he felt himself heaving a sigh of relief as he saw his Sangeet approaching to the office door.

It did not take much time for Roshen to get used in the environment. Apart from the introduction, the first day was full of formalities which any newcomer had to do after joining, like filling up joining form, submission of a copy of PAN card and passport, filling up the application for a new bank account where all his salary would go on every first Monday of the month. *Thirty-two thousand six hundred fifty seven each month, not bad!*

"There is nothing much to do. This current project at Gujarat refinery is about to end, and for the next few days, all you have to do is to crosscheck and analyze the accounts in our procurement department." Roshen heard his boss saying after he was introduced to everyone in the office.

Why the hell you appointed me when you don't have anything for me, Roshen thought. He felt awkward in front of his boss. This was because of the fact that the clothes which his boss was wearing were kind of funny. His boss, Mr. Tiwari, was more than forty years old and was wearing his pants way higher than they should have been. The top two buttons of his shirt were open, showing large hair on his chest and after every few moments he was adjusting his groin the way Sachin Tendulkar does before taking guard. *This old jerk cannot iron his cloths and why he wears a shirt, with two buttons open and such high pants, it is hardly visible anyways.*

There were six other persons in the same room where he was given a seat and two of them were girls. Roshen was more qualified than all of them but was least experienced one. He was introduced to each by one person from HR department but as soon as he was introduced, he forgot their names except the two female colleagues, Kriti and Neha. Neha was married as her looks appearance suggested and was busy with her work. She was least interested in talking to some new person in the office. When Roshen offered her his hand, she barely touched it and got back to the work with a smile and '*got to meet deadlines*' look. *Her ass is on fire*, Roshen thought.

However Kriti was completely opposite. She was neither married nor busy in any work. She was chatting with people all over the office and Roshen hardly saw her doing anything the whole day.

By the time Roshen came back to the apartment, it was seven in the evening. Abhi was talking to a man at the door about some property case. The man looked at Roshen but Roshen went straight to his room. For a moment he wondered what case they were talking about but as soon as he started chatting with Abhi after the man left, he forgot about it. Abhi asked him about his day and Roshen was more than interested in talking about his first day to his new friend.

"Typical office, twenty percent people do eighty percent of work and the rest either just fool around or get them involved in office politics." declared Abhi when he felt Roshen was almost done.

"What do you know about offices? Have you been working in many offices all these years?"

"Come on dude, I know them well and that's why I hate to work for these multinationals. They don't have any real job for us. We just work for the sake of some money. No offence, but your dad is a govt. employee naa, go and ask him what difference he has made in this world in his job."

"May be not, but what is the deal, he has made a lot of difference in his own world and that is what matters. These companies need someone to work for them and we need something to do so that we can live. A simple give and take relationship, isn't it?" Roshen was now in a mood to argue as he was feeling insulted when Abhi referred to his father in-between but Abhi got the feeling that Roshen was hurt with his statement. He kept silent which cooled down Roshen as well.

"Are there any hot chicks in your office?" asked Abhi trying to divert Roshen's attention. He did not want to share anything personal.

"Yeah, one of them is quite pretty. She has also recently joined and is junior to me. But I don't know her name yet."

"You will soon know. Pretty faces can't hide themselves for long. I am sure lot of people in the office must be trying for her." Abhi declared as if he was some kind of stud.

"So would I." Roshen winked at Abhi this time when they heard a knock on the door. It was a tiffinwalah with two boxes Abhi had ordered earlier that day. Roshen was not much surprised this time because by now he was getting used to Abhi's this generosity.

Both kept on talking till midnight and then had dinner and this conversation in Roshen's room. It was about 10' clock when Abhi finished telling a story about how he almost got expelled from his college along with his few friends when he threw a bottle of beer at a professor when inebriated, but before he could finish this one, he realized that Roshen was fast asleep. He saw, it was raining outside. He was feeling a little cold. He pulled out a blanket from Roshen's luggage and covered him. He himself wore a jacket and opened a new packet of cigarettes. He pulled one out and went in the balcony where he could feel the tiny drops falling on him intermittently. It was one of the very few times in his life when he was thinking about his past instead of living in present and somehow, Roshen was reminding him of an old Abhi.

RANJIT YASHWARDHAN

Ranjit Yashwardhan walked across the hallway in the house which looked more like a palace and entered his study, which had earlier belonged to his elder brother, Rakesh Yashwardhan, before his death. It was a magnificent room lit with many lamps but all this illumination could not match the darkness inside Ranjit. Even at this age, he was feeling like a tired man. He had always tried to get everything he wanted but he was still feeling that he had reached a point from where he had started. Walking across the room, he switched off most of the lights. He did not want anyone to disturb him. The events outside were disturbing him enough already.

I had to kill my brother for all this but still I could not get it.

Huge portraits at the walls were staring at him and even in the dark room; he could not imagine that he was alone. The fact that he had killed his brother for the property, disturbed him a lot but the fact that it served no purpose, made things even worse. *Rakesh was going to die anyways; I just helped him get there faster.*

All these years Ranjit had never been the biggest fan of his elder brother but the element of guilt never disappeared. He tried to console himself by telling himself that even the doctors said that his brother had a completely natural death but the drama unleashed just two days after his death made all his efforts futile. *How many sins a man commits in his life!* How the hell was he supposed to know that Rakesh Yashwardhan was secretly married to a girl who was half of his age? And what a witch, she never showed up when Rakesh was alive and turned up just after his death, when everything was eventually going to be effectively mine.

All these years Ranjit had seen his elder brother wasting all the money their forefathers left. Rakesh gave away their palace to the Government without flinching, a huge amount of their property was seized and he did not blink, he started spending money like anything and whenever Ranjit tried to take control he was made to look like a silly young bachelor who did not know how to handle money matters. But even in those altercations between then, family values always prevailed. Ranjit never went against any decision Rakesh made. He always followed his father's wish to follow whatever Rakesh told him to do. Ranjit was never into the core of the dealings but the small investments he made in estate and funds always paid off. He had more business acumen than his elder brother and he always felt that he should be the one taking important decisions, not Rakesh.

Ranjit stood up and went towards the corner of the room where there was a small bar which contained a great collection of expensive wines he did not know much about. All he knew was that Rakesh was very proud of this collection. *What a boozer he was.* He poured a red wine in a glass and sat down on the chair where the bartender was supposed to sit. He took the first sip and winced as if he had glasses cutting him from inside his throat. Ranjit never liked the taste of a wine but still he was there, drinking and waiting for someone.

"She is not coming." A remote voice came from a person who just entered the room. The voice was very faint. Ranjit doubted that he heard it right.

"What are you saying?" Ranjit asked after clearing his throat a few times. The person who came with the news was now standing in front of him. He was Ranjit's lawyer, Tapan.

"Yes, I just called her. She refused to see you. Said that she will only talk in the court."

"What should we make of this statement?"

"Two things, first of all, if she says that she wants to see us in the court that means she has some substantial proof to show."

"If that's true, it becomes more important to meet her."

"That is the second thing, if she does not come to us; we can bring her here by force."

"No, we won't do that. We would give her a surprise, at her house. But before that, I want Bhupendra Singh with me. Make arrangements to bring him out of the jail." Ranjit ordered with a regal attitude. He was now determined that he would not squander the chance to get this property in any case. *I am the one who deserves it all and I will get it, all.*

LOVE STORY 1

It is a normal human tendency to want to improve things even after the point they cannot be improved further. The person who had climbed all the way to Mount Everest must have stretched his hands to reach higher. The same was the case with Roshen. A new job, a good friend and freedom made him looking for more and this time he was looking for what Abhi would have considered troublesome, a relationship.

Roshen was never the kind of person who had lots of affairs. All his life, he had been trying to get good marks in studies. After completing his studies, he struggled to get a good job to eventually fulfill what his family had expected from him. Although in-between he had his own share of feelings for other girls. He had a great crush on a girl in his college days. He even went on to propose to her but got rejected straightaway. He always consoled himself that one day when he got good job; there would be a lot of girls lined up for him. Now when he finally had a job, his desires were aroused. He looked around and found the best opportunity in the girl in his own office, Kriti.

Kriti was no doubt a beautiful girl but when Roshen first saw her, she was gossiping with some colleagues and the centre of attraction of the whole group. As a newcomer Roshen felt like he was left out of all this fun, but when Roshen started interacting with her, she came across as a very friendly person. She was a chatterbox always full of stories and with most of the persons in office fed up with her stories, she found a good listener in Roshen. Things started quite formally between them with things like exchanging a pen and Roshen asking for help about silly things. As a newcomer, he had the privilege to ask those silly things and slowly he developed a habit of always finding something to start a conversation. Kriti always came up with some story which all the people in the room had already heard several times but Roshen always found them amusing. Within a few days, he started feeling attracted towards her without realizing what he was getting into.

Kriti always came about half an hour earlier than the scheduled time. Her sister used to drop her. Since her sister's office started bit earlier Kriti was always there before the actual time. Roshen found an opportunity to come and flirt when no one was there in the office to disturb them. So he also started coming early. When Kriti asked him why he came early he gave her most stupid reason that he liked his job a lot and wanted to learn it fast. Kriti also found his company better than getting bored alone so she never complained. However, somewhere inside, she started to realize that Roshen might be having feelings for her.

".............so they both had to live together, forever, knowing that they both love each other but they cannot kiss because if they kiss, they both would die. What an irony, I could never do that. I would rather kiss and die."

Kriti finished one of her stories which she had told many times to other persons in the office but was completely new to Roshen, who was continuously staring at her without blinking. For a moment, Roshen felt he should move ahead and kiss her but before he could do anything, he heard Kriti shouting,

"Hello, story is over. Were you even listening?"

"Oh yes, I guess I was lost in the story. It was wonderful." Roshen managed to hide his embarrassment for the moment.

"You know I have told this story so many times but I never had so much fun telling this to anyone. You are really cute." Said Kriti and stood up to get busy in some other work while Roshen was not even listening. He kept looking at Kriti while she was working. For the first time, he was having difficulty in looking away from her he was so much attracted towards her. Roshen remembered the last time it happened when he was in college and the thought that he had been rejected the last time, made him a little self-conscious. He wanted to get closer to Kriti and this time he wanted to do it perfectly.

But Roshen had many problems in his way. For Kriti, he was still just a friend. Also apart from about half an hour in the morning when they were alone, all the time they had a cluster of colleagues surrounding them. Though they both had ample amount of spare time in the office Kriti was always busy chatting with someone and as Roshen was still new there, he could not afford to be very late with his jobs. But he found great solace in the fact that Kriti was in front of his eyes for most of the day. He was also struggling to hide his feelings from Abhi. Many a times he thought of telling him but somehow Abhi always discouraged him.

"Have you ever been in love Abhi?" asked Roshen one evening after both had finished two beers each.

"What!"

"Love, I said love, L...O....V...E" Roshen spoke each letter trying to make it look funny.

"Chill dude, what's the deal?"

"Nothing, just asked. You had girlfriends na, weren't you serious about any of them?"

"You ask a lot of questions."

"But you never answer" Snapped Roshen.

"Yeah, I had many girlfriends and you know what, I have never been in love with anyone. I make girlfriends, date them, have fun but somehow after some time, they start repelling me."

Roshen opened his mouth to say something but Abhi stopped him,

"No, I am not gay"

"Come on dude, there must have been someone"

"Seriously, what is the problem with you? Why are you having this mentality of shrinking yourself in your own diminutive world where all you care for a secure job for you, a beautiful wife with some children who will play in a garden and you will read your fucking newspaper with a cup of tea your wife would be serving and then you would comment on some sucking news that this world is full of shit and needs a change. Tell me who in this world cannot do that. All you need is to find some bullshit job, then a girl, who is not defected by-the-way, ability to produce sperms and, money to buy your idiot newspaper. Look outside man, this whole world is waiting for someone to be conquered. But instead you want to fall in love and be the goat in the flock, just because it is easy." Beer was making him express his feelings in a way which Roshen found arrogant.

"Do you think it was easy? Dude, it is easy for you because you have a rich family. I have struggled to get this job. I don't get money from my family fund. I am here after lot of efforts and I am proud of the fact that I have survived in this world where people kill each other for the sake of money. I am successful and now I deserve a peaceful life in the future."

"Look, here is the difference, you are living your life to survive and I am living it for fun. All the time you were trying to make your future beautiful complaining about your past but I am living in present. I don't want to remember my past and I don't care what will happen next."

"Then one day you will regret your attitude."

"May be, but I know I will never complain about my past and I guess I am this much able that getting a job won't be a problem for me even if my family funds dry up. But I don't want a job; I want to do something different. I am unemployed by choice, not by chance."

"And what on the earth that different thing would be?"

"I don't know but I will do it one day. Anyways, you should sleep now. It is already too late and you have a job to survive tomorrow. So, good night!" Abhi started to get up leaving Roshen again with his questions alone. Neither of them was feeling sleepy but their conversation had reached a point where Abhi did not want to talk anything. Roshen also did not push him much. He had a lot more to think; about his past, about his future, about Kriti.

LOVE STORY 2

There is a difference between becoming friends with someone and making someone a friend. Becoming friends is an inadvertent thing which is most likely to happen between two people with similar interests or nature or by a mutual liking. However making someone a friend needs efforts. To make someone a friend can be very easy sometimes and can be difficult as it was in Roshen's case.

Roshen was now trying everything to impress Kriti. He started to dress even more tidily. He started coming early so that he could get time to talk to her. He was also spending lot of money on her in the canteen and sometimes with occasional small surprise parties in office. Though Kriti was taking a lot of time before she could start talking on personal things with him slowly his efforts were paying off. Initially when Roshen came early in the office, he was just someone with whom she could spend her time but after some time, Kriti started waiting for him. Initially when Roshen offered her lunch from his plate, she was shy to take it, but after some time they started fighting for each-other's food. Roshen's nice behavior was paying off and he was happy.

"Do you have a girlfriend?" One day Kriti asked Roshen in the morning when there was no one to overhear.

"Nah, but I am looking for one." Roshen sounded both shy and proud at the same time.

"I can't believe that you don't have a girlfriend, I mean you are good looking, sophisticated and intelligent. Any girl would be lucky to have you as her boyfriend."

"Really!" Roshen was again both surprised and happy with her comment.

For a moment Roshen thought of asking Kriti 'Would you feel lucky to be my girlfriend?' but he thought waiting for some more time would be a more appropriate thing. Though they were friends but he still was nervous to say those words. Should I say it now, how should I say it, how she may react? There were a lot of questions and the worst part was, Roshen did not know the answers. Time was running and he knew that he must look around for those answers.

"What would you do if you ever fall in love with a girl?" Roshen asked Abhi that evening to find some suggestions.

"Don't you start again dude. You know me; I am not going to fall in love, if I do something in love that would be rising up." Abhi winked but Roshen definitely didn't like his joke.

"Don't tell me that you can never fall in love. Everybody does and don't say that there isn't the slightest chance that you can love someone."

"Ok, what's the deal even if I do?"

"What would you do then?"

"I would tell that girl that I love her."

"And how exactly will you tell her?"

"Dude, God has given me mouth so I can speak."

"So you would just go and tell a girl that you love her without making her a friend or trying anything. Any girl in the world won't say 'Yes' to your proposal."

"First of all, I can't love any girl without knowing her, and to know her, I need to be friends with her. And when I would feel that I love her, there is no problem in saying that when she is my friend. It's simple."

Again, no help from Abhi. Roshen was disappointed with the way Abhi said he would do things. *So I have to think it myself.*

Roshen decided he would first try to know what Kriti thought about him. That was not a difficult thing. *If you want to know what a girl thinks about you, invite her for dinner alone. If she comes, that means she trusts you and in that case, you can be fifty percent assured that she likes you.* Roshen remembered hearing those sentences somewhere and thought that would be wise a thing to do. If she comes to dinner, I would propose to her there with a gift, Perfect.

Roshen chose Saturday to ask her to come with him for dinner because the next day being a holiday, he thought it would be easy to convince her. He decided to ask her in the morning only because it would give Kriti enough time to adjust things if she had any further appointments.

So Roshen, after deciding everything, reached more than forty minutes early in the office knowing that he would have to wait for

Kriti, but he was so excited that he could not stop himself from coming so early. He was waiting for her anxiously, looking his watch after every one or two minutes but time kept on passing and his heart went on drowning. Soon it was more than five minutes past the time she used to come, but there was no sign of her. Roshen was now half expecting her to come at the office timing but she did not show up.

It proved to be the longest day in the office for Roshen. All his plans were shattered and he was rendered alone with his files and papers on his desk. He tried to contact Kriti on her cell phone but it was switched off. He asked his colleagues about her but no one had any clue. He even asked Neha, whom he almost never talked to but got the same response. *Why this day, she could have taken leave on any other day of the year, but why today.* Roshen knew that after this day, next Saturday is seven days far and he was not sure whether he wanted to wait this long.

After coming back from the office, Roshen spent the most boring weekend since he came here. He tried to call Kriti many times but her phone was always switched off. *What the hell is she doing?* Abhi asked him to take dinner outside on the Saturday night and then for lunch next day but Roshen refused both the times. He also had a small fight with Abhi when he insisted. Eventually Abhi had to go alone and when he came back with beers, he was so angry that he did not ask Roshen whether he wanted one or not. Roshen was sleeping or reading some novel for most of the time but his thoughts were concentrated on Kriti. He was dying to go to office on Monday and talk to her.

Kriti did not come to office on Monday either. It was tough for Roshen. Somehow he spent the whole day. On Tuesday, he decided not to go early there and when he reached the office, Kriti was already there but busy in her work which was very unusual.

When Roshen passed Kriti's table, he kept staring towards her but Kriti did not even glance at him. Roshen was highly surprised. He came back, leaned on her table and tried to start a conversation,

"Hey, how are you?"

"Fine." Kriti looked at him for a moment and then made herself busy in her work again.

"What happened? Why didn't you come to office yesterday?" Roshen said. He did not expect that kind of response from Kriti.

"Was busy." Kriti again gave a short response and got back to her work. Roshen felt slightly embarrassed when he saw that Neha was looking at him. *What's her problem?* Roshen came back to his table to avoid that embarrassment.

That whole day Kriti did not talk to anyone. Roshen observed her expecting that she would come and talk to him, but she never did. When office was finally over, Roshen approached her when she was about to leave.

"Why are you so sad today?"

"It's nothing, just had a lot of work." Kriti was not looking into his eyes.

"I think you are angry with me."

"No, what makes you think so?" she now looked at Roshen.

"Then why are you trying to avoid me?"

"There is nothing like that. Actually I am in a kind of bad mood today."

"Why? What happened?"

"Nothing, I have to go now. See you tomorrow, and don't make me wait like today. Bye." Kriti said with a faint smile as she saw her sister coming.

"Bye." Roshen slowly said. His mood was lighter after this conversation. *Finally I will talk to her tomorrow morning.*

That night Roshen had dinner with Abhi in a restaurant. Abhi was still a little upset about the previous day but it took only two bottles of beer and a packet of cigarettes to cheer him up. The night passed quickly and it was morning again. Roshen was again with Kriti in the office.

"Why are you behaving like that? Tell me if something has happened." Roshen was finding it difficult to cope with Kriti's behavior when she was talking to him as if she was giving an interview. Only answering what Roshen was asking and speaking only when it was necessary. The office was about to start in few minutes and yet, Kriti was not really in a mood to talk.

"Nothing has happened. I am completely fine."

When girls say that, it always means they are not fine and something has happened.

"Won't you even tell me? Don't you consider me a friend? If that's the way you treat me, I don't really want to talk to you." *Emotional blackmailing,* Roshen hoped it would work.

"No, in fact you are one of my closest friends, I can tell you anything."

"Then why aren't you telling me what happened?" Roshen's tactics were working.

"Actually my boyfriend broke up with me; that's why I am upset."

Roshen was stunned to hear those words. He did not know what to say, he was confused. He could be sad knowing that just few days back, when he was dreaming of Kriti, she had a boyfriend or he could be happy knowing that she broke up with her boyfriend and now he had a chance. Things were more complicated than Roshen thought they were.

"Don't worry, everything will be all right." Roshen said. He saw some people coming in and thought it would be better to be seen working in front of them. "We should work now. Don't be upset, may be you don't have a boyfriend now, you always have friends who care for you. Never think you are alone, and even if you are, someone is always there waiting for you to be alone so that he can find your company."

Kriti smiled and whispered 'Thanks' to Roshen, who was now going back to his table.

HAPPY DIWALI

"Abhi, where are you?"

Roshen started shouting even before he entered the apartment. He was very excited about his first trip home. He had got a vacation of a full week for Diwali and was leaving for home the next morning. He had a full list of gifts to buy for his parents and cousins. Even that day he came early from office and was calling Abhi as they he promised him that he would help him with shopping and then they both would go and have some drink as for the next seven days, Roshen would not be able to drink in his home.

"Wait a minute" Abhi shouted from inside. Apparently he was getting ready. After few minutes, when Abhi opened the door, he was all dressed up. Abhi was surprisingly fast in getting ready whenever they had plans to go outside. He would always put on a Tee shirt and Jeans with sandals and get going. Roshen was however absolutely the opposite. He used lotions, creams, hair oils, deodorants whenever getting ready. This always irritated Abhi because of the time Roshen used to take and Roshen was irritated because without any efforts, Abhi always managed to look smart.

"So where is your list? We should get going or we may end up sleeping in the market only." Abhi said as he started walking towards the door.

"I won't let you sleep till I buy everything written here. Don't worry, I have planned everything. And one more thing, I won't drink much today, just a beer. I am not feeling like having a lot." Roshen kept speaking as they walked out of apartment and locked the door.

It took them all the evening to buy those items and Abhi proved to be a great help. He selected a very handsome suit for Roshen's father, though the price of the suit made Roshen sweat for a moment. They had an argument about the choice of earrings but Abhi managed to buy what he wanted by saying that he knows more about girly stuff than Roshen. Roshen eventually had his say when they were buying saris and he bought two because for the first time Abhi was approving his choice. On the way back, Abhi bought two beers without talking to Roshen.

"What are you doing this Diwali?" Roshen asked as Abhi turned the key into the keyhole to open the door.

"I have plans."

"What plans, are you not going home?"

"Who said I am not going. Of course I am, don't make up things like that on your own."

Roshen felt embarrassed for a moment. He never imagined Abhi with a family. He would rather have a party with friends instead of having dinner with someone he could not impress. Roshen sometimes felt sorry for Abhi for the kind of person he was but sometimes he was jealous as well, as he never saw Abhi sad or sentimental or crying about things. He was always fond of Abhi whenever he was alone and he wondered how much his family would be missing him.

Roshen was staring at Abhi which Abhi made feel awkward. He punched slowly at Roshen's shoulder and asked,

"What happened?"

"This is for you." Roshen took a small silver colored box out of his pocket and handed it over to him.

"What is this?" Abhi looked surprised. He had surprised Roshen so many times but it was the first time Roshen had given him something.

"How could I forget to gift my best friend something when I am buying gifts to everyone? Happy Diwali dude." Roshen smiled.

Abhi opened the box. It was a wrist watch, square shaped, silver body and black dial. It was shining in the dim lights of the hall.

"I liked this one a lot and I thought you would tell me to buy some other piece if I tell you, so I bought it without telling you." Roshen winked; a habit he learnt from Abhi.

"It's really beautiful. Thanks" Abhi was still surprised. He never thought that Roshen would buy him a gift. He took the watch out and wore it. He looked at his hand then turned around and disappeared in his room.

Roshen followed him in his room. He sensed that Abhi got somewhat sentimental at that moment. But as he walked inside the room, everything was normal. Abhi put the bottles aside and started to change. Roshen moved ahead and picked up one bottle. He saw Abhi's laptop which was lying on the floor. It was always on. Abhi was writing something. It was a story of a young boy who falls in love with his classmate. Roshen started reading it. Small incidents were expressed out very carefully in words; it reminded Roshen of his first crush. *Abhi is a good writer, hope he knows that.* After Abhi changed his clothes, he sat down with Roshen and opened the beer.

Soon the bottles were empty and both of them didn't feel anything. Abhi wanted more but he felt that Roshen might not want to drink so he didn't say anything. Roshen felt that Abhi was speaking very little that day compared to any other time when he just couldn't shut up.

"Is that your own story you are writing?" Roshen tried to make Abhi say something as beer was finished and it was getting boring anyways.

"Nah, just imagination"

"Then why don't you write your own story? You changed many girlfriends; you must be having some really good stories."

"Yeah, but I think my story is not something which I will write to sell to some creepy magazine. I don't like people judging me. If I am gonna write my story, I will write it for myself and I don't think right now I have that much material to write on that masterpiece." Abhi winked as if he had cracked a great joke but Roshen did not find it funny enough.

"So what would be your story like; love story or college life or on your family." Roshen tried to dig deep in Abhi's life.

"Don't know, I had small stories in my life but none of them make any sense. Look, right now my life is in middle of nowhere, so I don't know where those stories will lead."

So he realizes that he has screwed up his life, thought Roshen. He wondered when Abhi started screwing things up. He thought it would be better to ask indirectly.

"When did you start drinking?"

"When I was in eighth standard. I used to steal wine from my dad and then fill it in the water bottle and take it to school. With my one friend I used to drink it up. One day our class teacher caught us and told my dad. He beat me and sent me to boarding school. There I started drinking even more whenever I got the chance."

"Wow, your father must be shattered knowing that you drink."

"Nah, he never had time for me. He was always busy with his own life. He hardly used to come to see me even after I left home. I never missed him after his death." For the first time Abhi was sharing his personal life with Roshen.

"And your mom, what was her reaction?"

"She was no longer alive to show any reaction. She passed away when I was four. All the memories I have of her are in her pictures and paintings."

"Oh, I am sorry." Roshen was taken aback. He knew that Abhi's father had died some time ago but he never knew about his mother. *So what was the family he was talking about?*

"Don't be" Abhi continued,

"Even I have stopped being sorry about her. I may have all the money in the world, but I never got any family. Perhaps that's why I don't feel about the things in the way a normal person does. We cannot change some things even if we want to."

"Yeah, that's right."

"No, it's wrong. Everything is unevenly distributed in this world. People don't have the thing they need the most. I don't have parents and a screwed up person like me needs guidance more than anyone.

You don't have money when all you want is to earn money and live a stable life after getting married. We all need a little bit of love but nobody gets it from the right person. Perhaps God didn't have much time when he was writing the stories of our lives."

Abhi was being philosophical and Roshen started getting bored but he did not want to comment as Abhi was getting this much personal for the first time. Roshen closed his eyes and rested his head on the wall behind him. *Tomorrow was going to be a great day.*

Roshen went home and gave gifts to everyone. Everybody was happy. They were asking about his job and life and he was telling them how great it was. But his sister wasn't in a good mood. She started complaining about how long he had taken to come back home and that also for such a short period. He gave her gift but instead of being happy, his sister punched him on his shoulder; Then on his leg. *Ahh, what is she doing?* This time even harder in his stomach.

"Oh my God" he screamed and opened his eyes.

"Wake up. You are getting late."

It was Abhi. Roshen had slept on the floor that night all dressed up. He looked at his mobile and shouted again, "Shit, why didn't you wake me up early? Its five thirty already. My train will leave in forty minutes. Damn!"

"Don't talk and get going. I am not your alarm; even I woke up just now."

Roshen did not say a word and rushed to the bathroom.

"Don't waste your time in there, they have toilets in trains." Abhi shouted from outside.

When Roshen came from bathroom, Abhi was packing his cloths and gifts. It seemed like he was in a greater hurry than Roshen.

"Would you please not use your make-up for one day? There are no girls to flirt with in the train." Abhi said when he saw Roshen standing in front of the small mirror hanging on the wall.

"It's just a cream, not make-up" Shouted Roshen.

Within ten minutes Roshen was sitting in an auto rickshaw and Abhi bid him goodbye.

"Don't worry; you will reach the station in fifteen minutes." Said Abhi as the auto started. Roshen waved at him and auto started to move. Abhi also waved and started to walk towards his apartment which was going be lonely again for next few days.

Abhi came back in his room lost in thoughts. He tried to sleep but couldn't; for a moment he thought how good it would have been if he were in Roshen's place. He would be going home after a long time to see his family. He tried to fight his temptation to miss being in a family but the harder he tried, more difficult it became. He tried to recall memories of his mother but all he could picture was a little boy standing in a room with a small girl of his own age asking a question, the answer of which he never forgot,

"Will mumma ever come back?"

More tears started flowing and when he heard a reply that most certainly was not positive, his heart drowned after he saw the little girl's response. The little hope that innocence gave that child were crushed by an innocent nod of the other. Abhi could not restrain himself and picked up his phone to dial her number.

PRIYA

It is strange how people start to love things that are around them for long. Abhi had been staying in the same apartment for more than two years now and was familiar with each and everything inside. Apart from Roshen's room, the apartment was a complete mess. He had problem in moving around inside his room but whenever he was alone, only his room gave him the comfort he never got anywhere else. He knew each book that was kept on his bed. His old computer, which he had bought in his college days and which faced most of his experiments and was now hardly breathing; Abhi liked it so much that he never threw it away, however he never tried to use it or keep it away from dust because of laziness. The giant Monalisa, which he hung inverted the day he bought it, was his favorite thing in the room as it always reminded him of someone very special; he had spent a major part of his life with. Today after Roshen left, he was again noticing these things which always gave him company in his room.

The long strings of Abhi's thought were disrupted by sounds of somebody entering the apartment. From the footsteps, he reckoned it should be Roshen, *but how is it possible? He must be in the train or did he miss it?* He moved out of his room to check whether his intuition was right, he prayed not. As he stepped outside his room, he saw Roshen standing with his bags on either side of him.

"What happened, didn't you reach there in time?" Abhi was anxious to know as Roshen had left on time.

"I got stuck in the traffic." Roshen hardly managed to say. His voice clearly expressed how badly he wanted to be in that train.

"When I reached, the train was leaving. I tried to run but couldn't catch it." Roshen did not cry but tears were waiting on the verge of his eyes. Instead Roshen smiled and put them back.

Abhi suddenly felt strange. The way that room had felt in the last hour was terrible but he never wished Roshen to come back. He wanted him to catch the train. It took him some time to get Roshen turn to his normal self by his silly jokes and some old consoling dialogues and once he was done, he had things to do but now he knew Roshen would accompany him and he was more than happy.

"Where are we going?" Roshen was not in a mood to play. In fact it took a lot of efforts from Abhi to make him move. *'You have a heavier butt than other people,* was Abhi's remark when Roshen was reluctant to go with Abhi. But one thing that Roshen had learnt in his stay with Abhi was that it was very difficult to say 'No' to him. Abhi used to convince Roshen almost every time and Roshen never felt it was wrong as Abhi never sounded unreasonable.

"Do you know anything about paintings, if not; today you have a chance to learn art." Abhi was as usual oblique in his response.

Roshen preferred to keep silent. He just kept looking out of the auto as it was moving. He wanted to stare out of the window of the train that time. As the auto stopped outside their destination, he did not want to get going. It was a large building with no name on the front. On the three sides there were huge gardens where some painters were busy with their work and apart from one or two other people, those parks were empty. Art never interested Roshen even remotely and that sight made him more dull. Abhi entered feel Roshen followed him unwillingly. He was feeling that missing the train was not the only bad thing that day; *I would be tortured by some artist on his stupid artwork which could be anything but interesting.*

"Why do these artists always have long hair and beard? Is this some kind of character thing which makes them look impressive?" Roshen's irritation started showing in his comments, "May be they don't earn enough to manage their expenses of getting a haircut."

Abhi kept walking as they crossed a small canteen. A group of foreigners were talking on a table. They looked like students. A blonde waved at Abhi and he waved back with a smile and kept walking. *Nice girl*, Roshen thought. They reached an open space after crossing the canteen and then moved towards the left and entered a room from which a smell of roses wafted outside from incense sticks inside. Roshen entered the room behind Abhi. It was full of paintings on the walls. A few people were staring at the paintings one by one as if judging them. Around a table near the entrance were a few people talking. The chair in front of the table was empty and Roshen felt like sitting on it but the environment was completely alien for him and he did not dare. *Idiots, why is there a chair when nobody is sitting?*

"This is a charcoal painting with acrylic paints around the corners." A girl was describing some painting to a person who was listening as if she was telling Harry Potter story to a kid. *How can people be interested in this kind of stuff,* Roshen was wondering when Abhi tapped her shoulder from behind and she turned around to face them.

Roshen was stunned for a moment with the sparkling figure standing in front of him. The girl he was looking at was extremely charming. She was fair with big shining eyes and a face on which every line and every turn seemed carefully etched by a great artist. Long straight hair, falling on her shoulder were making that flawless figure look even more beautiful. *Now this is what I call art; No doubt that fellow showed a keen interest in every word she was saying.*

"So prince got time to come here. How lucky I am." That girl spoke to Abhi. Roshen was still thinking about how beautiful she was.

"Come on Priya, You know me. I don't like to attend these kinds of events."

So her name is Priya, Roshen was keeping the score.

"What events are you talking about Abhi? It is the first exhibition of my life and I want one person to be here but guess what, he does not like 'these kinds of events'. Was it so very difficult for you to come yesterday?"

"I am so sorry, I don't have any excuse, so as an apology, I will buy that painting of yours." Abhi said pointing towards a painting which seemed to Roshen nothing more than a naked man in a jungle. "But tell one thing, how come one flying leaf is exactly in a position which covers his thing?" Abhi almost forgot that Roshen was also there.

"I am not selling you any of these. I don't want any apology selling of my paintings. Now if I have permission, can we sit and talk?"

"Of course ma'am. Today I am all yours." Said Abhi as they started moving. Roshen did not know what to do. So he coughed aloud to get Abhi's attention. This time Abhi noticed him and felt awkward for in the last few moments he unknowingly ignored him completely. So he tried to make things up.

"By the way, this is Roshen, my friend."

Finally, Roshen thought.

Priya waved her hand and said "Hi."

"Hi" Roshen smiled and said when Abhi again started talking to her. They kept walking towards the canteen and Roshen was still wondering what Abhi was doing with such a beauty. *Absolute punk, can score any girl he wants.*

Soon they were sitting in the canteen far enough from the crowd with three cups of coffee and snacks. On the way to canteen, one more girl waved to Abhi. *Why only girls, no boys know him here*, Roshen wondered. From the conversation it appeared that both Priya and Abhi were very close to each other. They were fighting almost all the time but that was the kind of fight which is common among friends. For a moment Roshen missed Kriti.

"So Roshen, what do you do. Don't tell me you don't do anything, I hate hearing that from Abhi." Roshen was disturbed by an unexpected question from Priya when he was deep in his thoughts.

"Nah, I work in the accounts department of a multinational. Job is kind of monotonous but I like it."

"Why don't you tell Abhi to take up some job? I've been trying to convince him for last three years but he likes to live in his own world.

He always has a new explanation for not taking up a job."

For a moment Roshen felt proud of his job. He looked at Abhi and smiled as if he wanted to say, 'Look, there are people who think what I am doing is right and what you are doing is wrong.'

"I also want him to take up a job, but he never listens. I think he still lives in his wonderland."

"Wow, now you have his support as well. You guys are not real friends. Friends are supposed to be supportive about whatever I want to do. You should instead be saying 'go on dude, what you are doing is right.' But you are like parents, 'don't do that, do it this way.'" Abhi finally said when he had enough of them.

"So you think we all are idiots trying to make you do stupid things." Priya said in a slightly angry tone now.

"Ok, you want me to take up a job, I'll take up a job. Now are you happy?" Abhi said.

Roshen had seen Abhi surrender so quickly for the first time. He was really surprised to see how quickly he agreed when Priya told him to take a job.

"No, I am not happy. I'll be happy when you will actually start working. There is a company which deals in building power plants. I know the managing director of the electrical operations there. You go and give an interview there. I am sure you will get selected."

"Yeah, that would be great." Roshen said. He felt that he should not be just an observer in the discussion.

"What is so great about that? You are getting to do what you like. Priya is drawing naked men which by the way she likes. Then why am I the only one here who has to do what he doesn't like." Abhi was clearly annoyed by the thought of working.

"I am no Michelangelo who likes to draw naked men. This is art and if you don't understand it, don't comment."

Who the hell is Michelangelo, Roshen thought but did not ask. He was not even interested.

"Ok, I won't. But will you please come with us to 'Bachpan'?"

"Hmm, I have to think. It is really difficult to leave."

"What is Bachpan?" Roshen interrupted.

"It's my family." Abhi said with a smile. Again an oblique response, Roshen did not understand.

"It's an orphanage Abhi's father set up. Abhi loves going there. In fact he donates a lot of money there." Priya explained.

"As if you don't do anything for them." Abhi said loudly and turned to Roshen, "She is also going to donate all the money she earns from this exhibition." Abhi was not happy with the mention of money donation by him. And he was had his revenge by saying that Priya also did the same. Roshen felt so small before those two. He always knew that Abhi was a great guy but now he was feeling bad for himself.

"Come on, let's go now. I am sure you will have fun with the kids." Said Abhi tapping Roshen's back as he understood what he was thinking. This time Roshen asked himself whether he has any other choice and the answer was a big 'No'.

"I need to make some calls. You can wait here or see naked men in my paintings." Priya stood up.

"We will wait here." Snapped Roshen before Abhi could say anything. *Watching those paintings and getting tortured! It's better to wait with butt resting on a chair.*

After Priya left, Roshen got some air to breath. In her presence he felt rather shy. He did not want to say anything which might make him look stupid in front of a really beautiful girl he had just met. But now with Abhi, he was feeling more comfortable.

"So, is she also one of your girlfriends?"

"Priya! nooo way." Said Abhi with a long stretched 'No'. Roshen was surprised as anybody would consider himself lucky to have a girlfriend like her. "She is a very good friend. I know her since I was a child. She used to live in my neighborhood. We had a lot of fun together."

"So you have nothing else between you?" Roshen was trying to confirm everything before he could flirt with her. However he would never choose an unknown girl over such a good friend but *just in case*, he thought.

"Actually we have. She loves me. In fact at one point of time she proposed to me."

Roshen was stricken. Abhi rarely talked about any girls in his life but Roshen could barely imagine that such a beauty had proposed to him.

"Then, did you say 'No'?"

"I said 'Yes', but only if I will marry."

CRICKET MATCH

Sometimes it takes a long time to make someone a friend and sometimes you meet someone and somehow you instantly know that you have some connection with that person. Till Roshen was unaware that Priya loved Abhi he felt uncomfortable in front of her. But when Abhi told him everything, he no longer tried to impress her and suddenly that eased him a lot. He was again normal and found that Priya was also as good as Abhi, in making Roshen a friend. Priya was good fun to be with. While going to the orphanage, she sat with Roshen on the back seat of the car where they both kept chatting all the way while Abhi was enjoying his drive. It took them only fifteen minutes to reach their destination, 'Bachpan'.

"Look who is here." one boy from the bunch of kids who were playing with a ball, shouted as Abhi got down from the car.

Soon they were surrounded by a bunch of kids who were looking really happy to see Abhi. A few girls ran towards Priya and she started talking to them. But it was clear that Abhi was far more popular than Priya. Kids were calling him 'Abhi bhaiya'. Abhi was also giving individual attention to each of them. He knew the name of everyone. He was asking about their studies, giving hi-fives, telling jokes. Roshen also involved himself with the kids and it proved to be more fun than he had thought. Kids welcomed him also in their group as a new friend.

After talking to them, Roshen was feeling really happy. Abhi introduced him to the caretaker and left saying that he would come back in a few moments. The caretaker treated them with due respect. He showed Roshen the whole building. He told them that orphanage was built by Mr. Rakesh Yashwardhan who died few months back. After his death this property was under legal supervision. He also told Roshen that Abhi came there almost twice a week and spent time with kids. *So this is what he does when I am in office,* Roshen thought.

Roshen was having fun with those kids. They took him to their playground where some were playing cricket with a tennis ball. It was not a hot day with clouds disturbing sunlight and watching kids play made Roshen want to play with them. He wanted to ask Abhi but he had disappeared. Priya was also not there. For a moment Roshen felt nervous with the kids but then he saw both Abhi and Priya coming towards him. Seeing them walking together towards him made Roshen wonder whether any couple could look better.

"Where have you been?" Roshen asked as they came within audible distance.

"We were looking for you inside." said Priya, almost shouting.

"Actually the kids want us to play cricket with them. I thought you don't have anything to do so I said we would play. I hope you know how to play." Said Abhi with a smile.

"Ya, little bit." Said Roshen trying to hide his excitement. Cricket used to be his favorite game in school. "But what about you, you wanted to leave early." Roshen addressed Priya this time.

"She will watch us play." Abhi replied for her.

"Yeah, he convinced me to stay. And watching you people play and talking to kids is far better than explaining art to morons." Priya said with a smile so cute that it made both Abhi and Roshen smile.

Soon everything was set for the match. Both Abhi and Roshen were to captain one team each. Somehow eleven players were managed. Most of them were between ages eleven to fifteen. Abhi knew all of them very well so he chose a good team for himself while Roshen went with the suggestions he got from the kids there. It was decided to play a fifteen over match. Priya was the hypothetical referee and caretaker 'Babu' was the umpire. As Priya was about to toss the coin, Abhi stopped her and said,

"So what if you lose?"

"What do you mean?" Roshen was surprised.

"Come on, a match is no fun without something at stake. You must bet something to make it interesting."

"Money, hundred bucks?"

"Nah, something real."

"What can be more real than money?"

"I can tell you." Priya interrupted, apparently annoyed by them, "Whoever loses, will have to do whatever winner says. Is that okay?"

"Okay." said Abhi.

"Okay." said Roshen.

With those words, Priya tossed the coin in air. Abhi shouted 'Heads' but It was tails. Abhi's teammates looked disappointed while Roshen's team started shouting and they ran towards the pitch where bats were lying. Roshen remembered his school days when winning the toss always meant batting first, irrespective of the conditions.

Roshen could not stop himself from batting first. He was batting as an opener while Abhi gave the ball to a boy called Hari who was taller than Abhi himself. Priya sat on a chair under the shade of a tree with some kids of Roshen's team from where he could get a good view of what's going on the field while Hari took a long run-up to bowl the first ball to Roshen who was anxiously waiting to hit it after a long time.

Roshen missed the first ball completely. He never imagined that Hari could be that fast with the ball. Also it was a long time since he had played cricket. But he did not take long to get used to it and once he started hitting the ball, he was difficult to stop. He scored three boundaries in the next over and hit a six off Hari's ball in next over. The bowling was not bad but it was probably Roshen's day. Two players got out on the opposite side without making many runs but he kept playing the same way. His team scored fifty two runs in six overs when Abhi came to bowl himself.

Abhi was quite angry with the way game was going on. He was shouting at the fielders, telling them again and again to bowl better and when he felt that things won't change this way, he decided to bowl to Roshen himself who was having a great time. The first ball from Abhi was a leg spin which was very short for Roshen; he waited for it and pulled it for a six. *Very poor bowing Abhi,* he wanted to say. It was a nice change dominating a guy like Abhi.

The second ball was overpitched and received the same treatment, Six! Abhi looked frustrated while Roshen enjoyed this one a lot more. On the third ball, Roshen came ahead to hit it again for a six but the ball turned at the last moment and went through his wickets. He was bowled. Abhi was excited. He winked at Roshen who was now walking towards the tree now while a new batsman came to face the next ball from Abhi.

"You played well." Priya said when Roshen joined her.

"Thanks, its feeling great, playing after a long time."

"You can come with Abhi whenever you get time; he also loves playing a lot."

"Ya, I can see that, how deeply he is involved in the game." Roshen said looking at his players who were now starving for runs. Hari was back in bowling and took one more wicket.

"It is strange watching prince work so hard for something." Priya was more interested in Abhi who quickly picked up the ball and threw it towards pitch.

"I have heard people calling him prince before. Why do you call Abhi prince?" Roshen asked a question which he hadn't asked anyone before, not even Abhi.

"Because he is a prince." Priya quipped. Roshen looked at her in surprise. He always knew that Abhi belonged to a rich family but he had never imagined he would be a prince. Priya continued, "He belongs to the royal family. Of course they don't rule on anyone now but still people respect them and call him 'Prince Abhimanyu Yashwardhan'."

'Prince Abhimanyu Yashwardhan!' I have been living with a prince for so long and I didn't even know it. Roshen was stunned. He kept

on watching the match but his brain now was thinking something else. Abhi took one more wicket and Roshen's team was now struggling with eighty five runs for five wickets in eleven overs.

Why didn't he ever tell me? Roshen was now having trouble with the fact that he knew very little about the person he spent most of his time with. *I did not even know his name.* And how he was supposed to know when Abhi never talked about himself. They had arguments, long discussions but never on Abhi's life. Roshen was not talking to Priya now and she was busy chatting with a little girl. Meanwhile Roshen's player hit a six and one boundary in last the over and their score reached hundred and sixteen runs in fifteen overs and it was Roshen's turn to field.

Unlike Roshen, Abhi did not bat initially. He sent two other players on the crease. Roshen did not feel like bowling himself so he gave the ball to some other kid who his teammates claimed was a good bowler. The bowler was really good; he picked up a wicket in his first over and gave just five runs. Roshen did not bowl the next six overs even when things for his team were not going well. Abhi's team scored sixty runs in seven overs with the loss of just one wicket. Roshen wasn't thinking about the game but the plight of his team prompted him to bowl, though he did that with very little energy but yet, that amount was sufficient for those amateur kids.

Roshen bowled the eighth over of the innings and picked up two wickets; both well set batsmen were out in one over. After being hit for a boundary off the first ball, Roshen came back well in the over and was now feeling good after taking his revenge. His success in the first over made his concentration shift from Abhi back to the match. But his over prompted Abhi to come on to the crease.

Abhi was watchful for the first two overs. He took his time while

Roshen took one more wicket in his next over. Their score was now seventy four for four wickets in ten overs. Roshen realized that this was going to be a close match as Abhi was a better batsman than bowler.

Roshen did not come into ball again till last over. He had only one over left and he wanted to use it in the end. Abhi played some good shots including two consecutive boundaries while one more player of his team was bowled and the score was now one hundred and four runs and five wickets were gone. They needed thirteen runs in the last over which Roshen was going to ball with Abhi on strike. With a *'not so good'* player on the other side, it was proving to be the match between those two friends.

The first ball from Roshen was a short pitched one which struck Abhi on his thighs. Roshen was happy to throw a dot ball.

The Roshen tried to repeat what had happened with the first ball by throwing a short one again but this time Abhi got hold of it and pulled it, it was a misfield and ball went past the boundary line. Four! "Nice shot" Priya shouted and clapped sitting on her chair. Equation was *nine needed in four balls.*

The third ball was lot fuller and outside the off stump which Abhi missed completely. Now he was under pressure. *Nine runs were needed in just three balls now.*

The fourth ball was again outside the off stump but slightly overpitched. Abhi threw his bat on that one and got connected; the ball went for a long distance. Six! Abhi's players were shouting now. *Three needed of two balls now.* Roshen was tense, so was Abhi.

The fifth ball was again a dot. Roshen bowled full length and almost missed Abhi's stumps. Three needed of the last ball to win, two for a tie. Now everybody was watching closely. One ball, to decide the fate of the match. Roshen went back to take a long run-up for this one.

Abhi came slightly forward when Roshen was about to bowl. Roshen yorked this one in Abhi's feet. Abhi tried to drag the ball with him but failed. The ball eluded him and rattled the stumps. Abhi was bowled. He looked back in frustration but the match was over. Roshen's team won the match by two runs. Roshen started celebrating with his players by hugging and giving hi-fives. Now he almost forgot about what Priya had told him about Abhi. He had a nice day after missing the train. Met a beautiful girl, made friends with her, played cricket after a long time and almost single-handedly won the match and that also from Abhi. Abhi looked sad for a moment then he joined Priya and other players and was cheerful after some time.

"So, what do you want me to do?" Abhi asked Priya and Roshen.

"I don't have anything in mind. Can I use this power later?" Roshen asked, he was still in a mood of celebration. He had won to Abhi, which was enough for the moment.

"No, you..." Abhi was saying before he was interrupted by Priya,

"Yes, you can, but only when I am present."

Abhi did not oppose. He just smiled and said 'Okay'. Roshen was wondering why Abhi did not oppose Priya. The way Abhi behaved in front of her, Roshen wondered if he had feelings for her.

"Anyways, I have something for you." Priya said moving to Roshen. She had a smile on her face.

Roshen was surprised to hear that as he met her for the first time. *What could she possibly have for me?*

"What is that?" Roshen asked.

"Tickets, to your hometown." Said Priya, who had some papers in her hand. She smiled and put them in Roshen's hand. Roshen looked closely; it was ticket of a flight which was leaving in two hours. Roshen looked at Abhi who was also smiling behind Priya. There was no need to explain anything then.

VANDANA

"So what does this lady, Vandana do?" Ranjit asked his lawyer, Tapan when he was heading towards the house of the lady who claimed to be the widow of Rakesh Yashwardhan in a cab sitting with two other persons. One of them was the driver and the other was a key person for Ranjit, his old servant cum mate who, on many occasions, had threatened and beaten people up for him. And the lady he was going to meet, Vandana, was the one responsible for leaking the fact that Rakesh Yashwardhan had died without a will and now she was all set to get a big part of his property.

"Nothing actually. She moved in the city a few years back and since then she had been in touch with your brother. The house she is currently living in was given to her by Rakesh only. She is well educated and probably has many contacts in this city now." Tapan said while the person other than driver was listening to him as carefully as was Ranjit. He knew his job was just to scare this lady but he was interested in what was going on. Ranjit was also not surprised to hear that his brother had gifted a house to a girl as he himself had done that to two girls. There was a silence in the cab after he completed.

"I know it's none of my concern but I want to ask you one thing." Tapan said breaking the silence after few minutes.

"And that is..." Ranjit said.

"This property is worth more than a billion and even if you don't try, you will get a major part as you belong to royal family. Then why are you insisting on getting the whole property for yourself?" Tapan asked, a question that Ranjit could not answer.

After searching for words for next few seconds, he finally spoke,

"I should have got this property when my father died. But in his will, he gave everything to Rakesh. Since I was a bachelor and I loved my brother, I never asked for this property."

"What happened then?" Tapan was curious about every detail.

"I always thought that though I am not the official owner, I can make decisions but slowly I got to know that my brother wouldn't let me interfere in property matters. My decisions were always underestimated. I always knew if I had power, I could use this property to make a lot more money, but he kept on wasting it. He made a stupid orphanage in the middle of the city. If I were in his place, I would have built a mall. If I will get this property, I am going to turn this palace into a heritage hotel."

Everybody was silent again. Tapan understood that Ranjit had a lot of plans for this property and the way he was speaking about it, his enthusiasm indicated that he would do anything to get this property. Soon there was a pause in his thoughts when the cab stopped in front of a house which looked as if it had recently been renovated. The driver waited in the cab while the three persons entered the house without knocking on the door which was not open but not bolted as well.

"Who are you?" Vandana stood up from the bed on which she was half asleep when she saw three strangers in three different kinds of attires entering in his house where she had lived alone for last few year but a few months back, she invited her brother to come and live with her. Unfortunately that day, he was out of station as well.

Vandana was frightened at the sight of three strange men approaching her and one of them clearly belonged to the royal family given the silk dress and necklaces he was wearing. Out of the other two, one was dressed a little formally and the other looked as if he was there to rob her. *I don't have anything to rob in here yet, but soon I will become the queen.*

"Don't worry; we are not going to kill you." Ranjit said intentionally using the word '*kill*' in his first sentence which was more than sufficient to scare a woman in front of three strangers.

"That is if you cooperate with us." Tapan completed the sentence.

"What do you want?" Vandana's voice was showed that she was already scared. *There was no need to use force.*

"Just sign on these papers, this will make our job a little easier." Tapan said.

"What is written on them?" Vandana asked thinking how she could avoid these people.

"Just that you are not Rakesh's wife and you are taking your claim from his properly back."

"No way, I have proof. I have photographs and certificates. There is no way I am signing these papers." For the first time in the last few minutes Vandana with confidence but she did not know that she was talking to people who did not like to hear a 'No'.

"We will give you whatever you want. Money is not a problem for us." Ranjit said. He wanted things to go as smoothly as possible.

"Still no." Vandana grew in confidence when Ranjit spoke softly.

Ranjit signaled to the third man who was standing silently till now to take charge of things. The man, Bhupendra, moved forward, took the papers from Tapan and handed them over to Vandana. Vandana took them and kept staring into his eyes, a look that stated that she was not going to sign. After waiting for a few seconds, Bhupendra took a gun out of the pocket of his 'Kurta' and pointed it towards Vandana,

"Trust me; you don't have any other option." Ranjit said again in a soft voice but this time, it made Vandana realize how right he was.

INTERVIEW

A person becomes happy when he wants something and gets it, he can be happy when he never thinks of a thing and gets it. But the way he feels when he desperately does not want a thing and it keeps on chasing him, is really difficult to explain. In a world where people were running all over, putting in all their efforts to get a job, Abhi was being chased by jobs. In all these years, he had put down a lot of job opportunities. People around him were tired of seeing him doing nothing but he never cared. All he cared about was not getting bored and he always found one thing or the other to keep himself involved.

When Priya set up an interview for him, she always knew that Abhi was not going to take that job or interview, so she decided to pick him up and take him to the venue of the interview herself. When she came to pick him up at his apartment early in the morning just two days after Diwali, the apartment was as usual, in a mess.

"What is all this. How do you live here" Were Priya's first words instead of any hi or hello. Abhi was playing some game on his laptop which annoyed her even more.

"Why are you not ready yet, or am I supposed to do that for you?" Priya tried to show that she was angry however she knew that she would find Abhi this way.

"Please do that for me. I know you are great." Abhi was still joking.

"Don't be smart. Just get ready in ten minutes." Priya said and started cleaning the room; she started by picking up old newspapers and plastic bags and throwing them in the trash can.

"What are you doing?" Abhi snatched one bag from her hand. He didn't like her cleaning the room.

"I am trying to make this room a better place to live in, and if you have a problem with that, you better go and get ready because I will keep doing that till you are ready." Priya said in a tone that of a school teacher which made Abhi start getting ready like a kid.

Abhi removed his tee and put a white shirt. He then thought for a moment before removing his jeans but Priya was all busy in cleaning the room, so without wasting time he changed his into a pair of neatly ironed trousers. Priya looked at her for a moment and smiled to herself. By the time Abhi wore a tie and shoes; his room was looking far better.

Diwali for Abhi was a regular day. He spent it with Priya while she showed him some of her paintings. Then he went to 'Bachpan' once again that week and had some fun with the kids. He also got a call from Roshen and he said that he will come two days later. Abhi never thought of going home. Last time Abhi visited there was when his father died. That time he saw his father's face after a long time but unlike usual, this time he didn't scold him which felt very bad as a change. Priya was with Abhi when his mother died, and she was with him when his father died as well. In the span of twenty two years between those deaths, their relation only grew stronger.

"Shall we go now?" Abhi was all ready and was really looked handsome.

"Of course sir." Priya was impressed with his get up. She had seen him that way after a real long time.

All the way to the interview, Abhi was wondering how to escape from this interview, but he knew that not taking this interview would annoy Priya a lot and he did not want that. So he decided to take the interview and then see what happens.

Priya dropped him outside the building and told him to get back to his apartment on his own. *So nice of you*, Abhi thought. As he reached the office, he was told to wait in the outer hall with several other candidates, who were neatly dressed like Abhi; but most of them were nervous and anxiously waiting for their turn, unlike him.

"How long have you been waiting for your turn?" Abhi started talking to the person sitting on the same sofa to pass time. He was looking quite nervous and his hands were playing with a file full of certificates in his hand.

"Not long, I came here fifteen minutes back and was told that my turn would come in some half an hour, so I guess it should be anytime now." He was getting bored and a conversation with Abhi was a welcome change for him.

"From where have you graduated?" Abhi asked as he could not think of anything else at the moment.

"I have done a diploma course and have been working with a company for last five years. What about you?"

"I have passed out from IIT Bombay."

This one sentence from Abhi made that person even more nervous. *He had a better chance, having passed out of such a prestigious institution.*

"Then you would easily get this job." His expression clearly expressed what he was not happy to put in words. His face suddenly made Abhi realize that if he gets selected and did not join, he would be wasting that post for some more deserving candidate. *I don't even want this job, how can I make some person I don't even know, miss something this big.*

Abhi suddenly decided something and got up to leave but then he thought of Priya, who wanted him to take this interview. He was in a dilemma. Suddenly a lady walked out of the room where the interview was going on and called;

"Mr. Abhimanyu, please go."

Abhi stood up and on the way to the interview, took his resume out from his file and tore it up. Throwing those pieces in the dustbin just outside the room and sliding the door open in one action, he said;

"May I come in sir?"

"Come in please." One of the three persons sitting inside the room on one side of a long table said. One of them was trying to arrange some papers and two were looking at Abhi as he walked into the room. Without saying any word, he sat on the chair in front of them. He was nervous now; *he had to not impress them anyhow.*

"You are Mr. Abhimanyu Yashwardhan. Am I right?" The same person said looking at a sheet of paper.

"Yes sir."

"Mr. Abhimanyu, will you give us your resume?"

"Sorry sir, I don't have a resume."

"Why?"

"There was no electricity outside so I couldn't take a print out." The lamest of excuses Abhi could think at the moment.

"Will you give us your photograph?" The interviewer was looking at him angrily now.

"I don't have a photo either." Abhi was desperate to do everything wrong in his interview.

"Its ok, we will manage." Said one of the persons sitting in the right corner.

"So Abhimanyu, tell us something about yourself." The same person spoke once again. He had already started getting irritated.

Abhi looked down for a moment. He could have spoken more than an hour to answer but this was not the time to speak. He waited for a moment and said,

"Sir, my name is Abhimanyu Yashwardhan."

After this sentence, he was silent again. Interviewers were eagerly waiting for him to say something but he didn't.

"Tell us more." One person finally spoke.

"Well, I have done my B. Tech. in electrical engineering." Abhi spoke another sentence and became silent.

"So what are you favorite subjects?" They now started to get bored and came to the point as fast as they could.

"I love Programming." Abhi said as he knew they are looking for electrical engineers, not programmers.

"Subjects in electrical mister. We are talking about your engineering here."

"Every subject sir, I like them equally whether it is control system or machines or transmission and distribution. You can ask anything sir." Said Abhi. *Ask anything sir, I am gonna give you the wrong answer.*

"Ok, then tell us what you know about transformers." The person in the corner asked, he looked like the subject expert.

Can write a whole book about transformers, Abhi thought. But the answer has to be different.

"Transformers have an outer canopy made of some metal, they use some kind of oil and we hear some sound when we go near them." An answer that a person who does not know any damn thing about transformers would have given.

"What is inside these transformers?"

"Oil..... And wires... I mean windings." Abhi said acting as if he had to think too much to extract those words from his memory.

"Windings, what windings?"

Again a simple question, Abhi thought. *There are normally two windings, primary and secondary; and in some special cases, tertiary.* But the answer again had to be different.

"Lots of windings sir," Abhi tried to show confidence in his wrong answer, "Primary, secondary, tertiary, quaternary... lots of windings."

By this time, the interviewers had decided that they were not going to select this guy. But they were still trying to extract some correct answer from him.

"Why are these transformer used in a circuit?"

"To save energy sir, they save energy in a circuit."

Completely wrong, in fact loss of some power happens inside them.

"Ok, then why is a Transformer called a 'Transformer'?"

"Sorry sir..." said Abhi as if he did not understand the question.

"Why is it called a 'Transformer', why not 'Prabhakar' or 'Dinakar'?" another person tried to explain the question.

"Because sir," Abhi was full of confidence now,

"Transformer was invented by a person named 'Transformer'." A joke that made Abhi himself smile.

"Mr. Abhimanyu" the person sitting in the middle said politely.

"Yes sir..."

"Get out."

"Thank you sir." Abhi said and stood up from his chair happy with his performance. He danced a jig while walking out when he heard someone inside calling him a 'jerk'.

FAKE B'DAY PARTY

When Roshen came back from home, he realized how much life had changed since he moved into a new city. Here Roshen tasted a new flavor of the candy called 'life'. In office he had a crush on Kriti, which was a great feeling. At home he was drinking a beer daily and outside he was eating a lot of junk food and shopping a lot. Most of it however went into Abhi's account that had never ending funds; they always had enough to buy anything they wanted.

Meanwhile they bought a small refrigerator and they put it in Abhi's room. Every week they used to fill it up with few bottles of beer and after Roshen came back from office, they used to drink. Roshen sometimes saw Abhi talking on the phone about some case but whenever he tried to ask Abhi what it was about, Abhi just said it was a small property dispute and changed the subject. But as far as Roshen's life was concerned, everything was just about perfect and he was enjoying his new life with a cool, knowledgeable, unemployed and excessively rich roommate who was not just a roommate now but his best friend.

"Hello Roshen, where are you?" Abhi's voice was sounding completely different on the phone, "how come you called at this time?"

"I am in my office, listen; I need a big favor from you."

"Order me!" said Abhi in a sarcastic tone.

"I told you about that girl in my office, Kriti, she thinks it is my birthday today and expects a party."

"Wow, great. You must take her to dinner. You are cool man, and you are such a liar. It is not your birthday today, is it?"

"No, it's not, but when she came and hugged me to wish me a 'happy birthday', I could not say, NO."

"So what's the problem; let her think it's your birthday. Go out with her and have fun."

"Well, that's the part where I need help. Actually she thinks that party is at our apartment and all the arrangements are already made. She is coming with me from office so I cannot escape and you know that our apartment is all messed up."

"What is the deal with you, are you crazy? You are talking about a party in 4 hours for a girl whom you met just few days back."

There was a long pause and then Roshen spoke in a very soft voice which could easily be confused with that of some girl, "I never said that, but she is not some random girl, I think I am in love with her."

A long and awkward silence followed and Abhi suddenly felt his heart pounding, "oh, love... damn."

Next moment a smile appeared on his face and he said, "Don't worry dude, it is still 4 hours to go. I will do it all."

"Really, thanks a lot Abhi. Listen I told her that it is a small party and only my close friends are coming but no one from the office and you know, I don't have any friend except you outside the office. Sooo..."Roshen was stretching his so as long as he could.

"You come with your girl and join me and your close friends in the party. Bye"

That morning after office started, Roshen had a pleasant surprise when the girl of his dreams came and hugged him. Though he did not know the reason, he was least interested in it. But when Kriti wished him a 'happy birthday' after hugging him, he did not know how to react. Later he came to know that his friend Sangeet had told Kriti that it was Roshen's birthday and he was throwing a party at his apartment. He thought of telling Kriti that there was no such party but before that he talked to Abhi and after Abhi told him not to worry, he decided to give this lie a shot. But he was still cursing the moment he agreed in front of Kriti that it was his birthday. *I am a jerk, If I knew that Sangeet had told Kriti that it's my b'day, I would never have lied*, he thought.

While coming back to the apartment with Sangeet and Kriti for the party, Roshen was tense. After his conversation with Abhi, he tried to call him again few times to confirm that all the arrangements were made but the phone always went unanswered. He felt uneasy and his nervousness was quite visible on his face. *I should not have lied.* He left text massages telling Abhi that he would be reaching home soon, but never got any response.

Kriti soon noticed that Roshen was trying to avoid her. After she wished him a happy birthday, he hardly talked to her in the office which was quite unusual, although it was his shy behavior which made her like Roshen in the first place. Her first opinion about him was that of a dumb guy but that changed completely when she saw him working. Roshen was way faster and accurate than other accountants and though she was in junior to him unlike other guys, he never tried to flirt with her taking advantage of his position. And after all the things Roshen had been doing for her, she also started feeling for him in an unusual way.

As they reached the door of the apartment, Roshen was sweating. It was both heat and nervousness. The door was half open and a dim light was visible from outside. He pushed the door and entered and for a moment, he wondered whether he was in someone else's apartment. The hall which was completely empty except some trash had a dining table made of glass in the middle. On the dining table was a huge birthday cake, *fake birthday cake*. On the right hand side, there were four chairs and near the wall were arranged two long tables one of which was full of fast food and other had a closed bottle of wine and a few glasses. The only light came from candles. The rooms were locked and indicating that the party must stay limited to this hall. Rooms are still a mess. Roshen had never celebrated a real birthday party this way.

When he had a close look at the guests, they were five. One was the person he saw talking to Abhi in the apartment earlier, one was his own 'tiffinwalah' who was wearing an expensive suit; Priya who was looking beautiful as usual; one guy who used to live in the neighborhood and Abhi, who was certainly overdressed for the occasion in an Armani suit. As he entered, Abhi sang the birthday song and other persons followed him,

"Happy Birthday to you....

Happy Birthday to you....

Happy birthday dear Roshen......

Happy Birthday to you"

But Roshen, on the other hand, was surprised the way Abhi had arranged so much in such a small time and Sangeet was shocked to see the apartment. He was expecting that after finding out that there was no party, Kriti would be disappointed and then he would tell her that it was not even Roshen's birthday to make Roshen look like a fool. But he felt disappointed after seeing the way the party had been arranged and for a moment thought of the possibility that may be it really was Roshen's birthday. A prank he pulled out jokingly was now turned into classy birthday party which involved good food, a tasty cake and some slow music.

After about an hour everybody was preparing to leave. The tiffinwalah got a free suit and dinner to attend the party and the boy from the neighborhood drank a glass of wine and took a bottle of beer along with him. Abhi meanwhile took Roshen aside and asked him the whole deal about Kriti. Roshen told him the whole story how Sangeet got him in this situation and he had been too foolish to admit it was not his birthday.

Abhi had a close look at Kriti, she was charming. She wore a black dress which was certainly not appropriate to wear at a workplace. It was not too ostentatious but exposed her body. She kept talking all the way in the party to either Sangeet or Roshen but Abhi observed that she was also carefully watching what other people were doing in the party.

When Roshen cut the cake, Kriti was the first person he offered that cake to. Abhi felt a little hurt by that as he was expecting that he would be the one to get first piece. Abhi did not really like Kriti but he did not want to be too judgmental about her in the first meeting. He said to Roshen after he completed his story,

"Listen, you got to tell her the truth if you really love her. And you better do this today only or it would be some big problem."

"I want to, but Sangeet won't leave her alone for a moment and I am still afraid that he knows that it's not my birthday. What if he tells her that?"

"He most certainly will; but you got to tell her that before he does, and don't worry, I will take care of him."

"I don't have any idea how to do this."

"I can't help you with that. You just give me Sangeet's phone number; I am leaving you guys alone." Abhi waved towards Priya who was standing alone in a corner with a glass of wine with cold drink in it. *She is more beautiful than Kriti*, thought Roshen for a moment as he saw Priya. He had so much on his mind that night that he hardly noticed her in the party.

"Thanks a lot Abhi. Anyways, how is Priya doing?"

"Awesome, she is with me!" Abhi winked and left the apartment while Priya also left after him.

While Roshen, Sangeet and Kriti were enjoying snacks after Abhi left; Sangeet received a text message. Then he went outside to call someone and a few minutes later he came rushing inside and apologized to Roshen and said there was an emergency and he needed to leave. At that time Kriti had gone to the washroom.

"As you wish dude" said Roshen who was quite happy to see that. *How does Abhi do that? Is he a magician or something?*

When Kriti came back, everybody was gone except Roshen. Most of the candles had gone out by that time so the light was even dimmer. The music was still on. A part of cake was waiting on the table and some snacks and a half full bottle of wine were among the leftovers. Roshen was sitting on a chair near the cake, preparing a speech about how he was going to tell Kriti the truth.

"Where is everybody? And where is Sangeet?" Kriti said when she saw Roshen sitting alone.

"Everybody has left. Sangeet had some emergency, was in a kind of hurry."

"Then I should also leave now." said Kriti, who, no doubt, had a nice time with Roshen in the party.

"Yeah, but who would finish the cake now?"

"I am sure you can do that. This little belly of yours has a lot of space inside."

"Hmm, listen, I need to tell you something." Roshen said but he felt that he was suddenly falling short of words. He was quite nervous about how Kriti would react. For a moment he wondered if he could escape all this. But soon he decided that he needed to tell her. With his eyes looking away from Kriti, he started speaking once again.

"Today is not my birthday. I arranged this whole party to spend some time with you."

There was a long pause, Kriti kept staring at him and Roshen, who had some long lines prepared, was also silent. He could not recall any of those lines. All the candles had burned out by now and the only light in the room was from the glass window which was so dim that they could hardly see each other's faces. And in the spur of the moment, Roshen heard himself saying,

"I love you."

Roshen suddenly felt that he had done something really stupid. His heart was pounding. He was looking away from Kriti and then he realized that all his plans to tell Kriti and convince her not to be angry went horribly wrong. *It would have been better if Sangeet had told her that.* But he mustered up all his courage once again, walked towards Kriti who still had no idea how to react. Roshen looked in her eyes now standing at a distance of few inches and for the first time that night, he said something with confidence.

"I don't know when it started. I don't even know what you think about me. I don't know whether we would be friends anymore or not, but I know that when I first saw you, I wanted to see you again. When I saw you the second time, I wanted to see you third time and now I want to see you every time I open my eyes. I know that I have never felt this way before and I know that I will never feel this way again ever in my life."

Kriti was certainly awestricken. The way Roshen said those lines was wonderful. After Roshen said all this, he moved an inch closer to her. She didn't utter a word but closed her eyes. Roshen kept moving even more close until their lips finally touched. It was a gentle touch but soon Kriti swung her head backwards. Roshen didn't move but looked at her. After a few seconds, Kriti came forward and touched Roshen's lips. This touch caused a sensation in Roshen's head. He moved further ahead and started rubbing his lips gently against hers. The friction between those pair of lips was really wonderful. After a few moments this rubbing grew even harder. Roshen felt her saliva which eased their motion and the sensation grew even more. It was going on just not on his lips but all over his senses. This went on for a few minutes until they were finally done with their kissing.

Kriti eventually moved backwards slowly, stared at Roshen for a moment and said, "I should go now."

Roshen was still thinking about the kiss. He wanted to kiss her again but was uncertain of what to say. He just nodded. Kriti crossed the hall, picked up her bag and moved towards the door. As she reached the door, she turned and smiled towards Roshen, "Good night, see you tomorrow in office."

Roshen smiled in turn and said "Good night."

When Abhi came back Roshen could not stop thanking him. He was thanking Abhi again and again who just smiled hand. He was feeling sleepy but pretended to listen patiently while lying on the bed in Roshen's room. Roshen was however going on changing his position with words sitting sometimes lying horizontally on the same bed. His story ended eventually and now he wanted Abhi to speak but Abhi did not say anything. After waiting for a few moments, Roshen spoke again,

"And how did you manage to keep Sangeet away? How did you pull that off?"

Abhi, who was barely listening by now, suddenly realized that Roshen had just asked some question.

"What, what did you say?"

"I said how you managed to keep Sangeet away. I was surprised when he said that he wanted to leave."

"First I was planning to wet his pants and then lock him in bathroom." Abhi paused for a moment and winked to Roshen who was looking at him quite impatiently.

"Then I though it wouldn't work, so I called Mike and gave him Sangeet's number. Mike apparently convinced him through his friend that his mother had a serious accident and was in hospital right now. That idiot bought it immediately and started running."

"Poor man, how could he believe him?" Roshen was now trying to settle down in his bed.

"Are you insane? Mike is a lawyer, an intelligent and professional liar. Pulling off such small pranks is nothing for him, plus he also knows legal things to clean the mess up if some problem comes." Abhi said.

"You are a magician. You can do anything." Roshen replied. He felt thankful to God that he had got a friend like Abhi.

Abhi smiled and closed his eyes. He was so tired by now that he slept within a few moments on Roshen's bed. Roshen also tried to sleep but he hardly could. He was now waiting for the next day when he would see the love of his life again.

A RELATIONSHIP

The most wonderful and irritating phase in love is that which comes at the beginning of the relationship, wonderful for lovers and irritating for their friends. It is a phase when you start knowing a person and most of the time, whatever you come to know about them, you find lovely. If your lover sings a song, he or she always has a great voice. If your lover laughs too much, he is funny; when someone else does that, they are dumb jokers. If the lover is sad, he is 'sentimental', when someone other is, he is 'depressing'.

Roshen was in the phase where he found Kriti *'a perfect girlfriend'*. To him, she was always telling stories therefore there was never a 'vacuum of words'. She worked in the same office and Roshen thought it great thing that she was always in his presence, though Abhi once warned him that it was not a very good idea to fall in love with a person you worked with.

"...and that stupid fellow was still flirting even when Kriti was trying to show that she wasn't interested. Eventually when he wouldn't let her go, I had to come and sit with her and then he finally got back to work." Roshen finished telling Abhi one of his '*office and Kriti*' stories while they were drinking beer. After that night, Kriti always came in their conversation which was quite obvious as Roshen was thinking about her 24x7 and Abhi was the only recipient of his thoughts. He could not talk about her with his office colleagues and Abhi was his hero after he helped him in his relationship.

Initially Abhi did not mind talking about Kriti but slowly he started getting irritated. Abhi found it very silly and when Roshen used to tell him every minute detail, it was too much to handle for him.

"So now you are her bodyguard, whenever someone tries to talk to her, you will come in between and stop that person."

"Don't you think it is my duty as her boyfriend?"

"You have other duties as well; you have a job where people expect you to do your work. Whenever you will go and protect her from your own colleagues, you will become a villain. And let me tell you, it is only okay until your boss does not know about that. Once he comes to know you will be in big trouble."

"Nothing will happen." Roshen did not find any argument against what Abhi was trying to say.

"I hope so; but be careful. You don't want too many enemies in office." Abhi quipped.

"Don't worry. I am having the time of my life and I am sure nothing would go wrong." Roshen said. He was texting along while talking to Abhi and whenever Abhi said something, he was looking at his cell phone. When Abhi noticed that, he got even more annoyed. He jumped and snatched his cell phone. Roshen tried to stop him but

Abhi was really fast. He saw the cell phone; Roshen was having a phone chat with Kriti.

"This is how we would talk now. All the time in the office you are with Kriti, you come here and talk about Kriti and when I will say something, you keep on chatting with her on your cellphone. Why are you talking to me?" Abhi said projecting Roshen's phone towards him.

"I was just telling her that I am feeling sleepy." Roshen gave a dumb reply.

"Ok, now you are telling her that you feel sleepy, and why you won't, I am a fucking boring person."

"Why are you talking like that?"

"Because you are behaving like that. I set up all the things for you and now I am the one who is suffering the most."

"'Suffering!' How on the earth you are 'suffering'?" Roshen was giving extra stress on word '*suffering*'.

"Leave it dude, you won't understand." Abhi said. He did not want any argument with Roshen but Roshen was still charged.

"Come on, tell me. It is not some theory of Einstein which I can't understand. You are the man with so many explanations for everything. You must be having one for this as well."

"No, I don't have any." Abhi wanted to finish this conversation as soon as possible. He was sensing that Roshen's tone was really angry. He did not like Abhi snatching his cell phone.

"Hmm, I guess I should sleep now." Roshen realized that there was no point arguing with Abhi and he also wanted to chat with Kriti and with Abhi around that was not possible. *She must be waiting for my message.*

After Roshen left, Abhi started smoking a cigarette but he was still thinking about Roshen. He certainly did not like the way Roshen's behavior had changed in the last few days. But he knew it was only the beginning, a lot more was still inside the box.

"Why did you break up with your boyfriend?" Roshen resisted this question for some days but eventually one morning, he asked Kriti when he saw her in a good mood.

"We were not good together; we were fighting most of the time. In fact we never loved each other; I tried my best to save this relationship but he wanted to break up."

"Do you still miss him?"

"Does it really matter when I am with you?" Said Kriti pressing his hand hard. A touch which reminded him of the kiss that night. After that night, they kissed each other whenever they got the chance but things never went any further.

The way things were going on in the office, nobody was happy except Roshen. People now noticed that he was spending a lot of time with Kriti and though they never told anyone about their relationship in the office, people had started to suspect already. Somebody noticed that they both came to the office early when nobody was there. Rumors about them caught fire and soon enough, Roshen's boss, Mr. Tiwari, heard that his new appointee was having an affair in the office. The direct impact of that was increased work load for Roshen.

"So Roshen, it's time for you to do some real work. I hope you have learnt how to work now." Tiwari said in his awkward 'Sachin' stance to Roshen one day.

"Definitely sir." Roshen sensed that his honeymoon period in office was about to end. But what could he say?

"So you take the files from Padelkar, I want you to take full responsibility of his job. Ask for every detail. He is going on a leave for fifteen days. You will work with him only when he comes. And yes, come and ask me directly if you face any kind of difficulty."

"Sure sir."

"You may leave now."

This brief conversation made a smooth going life of Roshen like hell. Padelkar was the busiest person in the accounts department. He was always the last person to leave the office. Roshen was not ready for that much work but he had no option. Things had started to change for Roshen.

ANOTHER DAY IN OFFICE

"Come on; let's have a cup of tea at least. You don't have even that much time for me."

"Ok, you wait for me in canteen; I am coming in two minutes."

"No, you finish your work and then we will go together."

"Ok, let's go." Said Roshen closing his register he was making some entries in.

This was the third time Kriti had asked him to go to canteen and after saying 'No' twice, Roshen, who was already lagging behind with his work, decided that now it's not possible for him to work further without a break. For the last two days he had not got enough time to talk to Kriti. Even in the morning, after chatting for ten minutes, Roshen started working and needless to say, his colleagues were a lot happier now.

"Why are you so busy these days?" Kriti asked while they were passing Neha's desk. She stared at Roshen for a moment. A look that was saying, *'So you are getting your dose now'*. Roshen saw her and thought it would be better to ignore her.

"Actually Padelkar is on leave and I have to look after his work. So I am hardly getting any time. But don't worry; he will come back in a few days."

"But why he is on leave?"

"One of his sisters is getting married, he told me. Sounded like he has many sisters."

"But why are you getting all the work? There are so many other people."

Roshen did not answer. *Perhaps Tiwari loves my ass.*

Roshen ordered a coffee for himself and tea for Kriti. Kriti said she would have some snacks also, so Roshen paid for them as well. Initially Kriti used to offer to pay but after Roshen insisted a few times, she stopped offering to pay. It was by default, Roshen, who would pay whenever they had something or spend on something when they were together. Roshen did not mind paying those bills given Abhi was paying for him and his expenses were balanced. In fact he was saving more than he had planned.

"I don't think they will let you breathe soon, when Padelkar will come, you would be given some other responsibility. It is always this way, the person who works more, gets even more to do."

"What can I do, I am a trainee, not even confirmed. I can't refuse to work."

"I know that. But when you are so busy, I feel lonely."

"Yeah, but we have no choice. Do we?" Roshen was trying to finish his coffee fast. He had to get back to work as soon as possible. Kriti, on the other hand, had all the time in the world and that reflected in the way she was having her tea. When Roshen was almost finished, she had barely touched her cup,

"I should go now. Have a lot of work pending."

"Sit here till I finish my tea, pleeessee." A long stretched 'please' made Roshen sit there but he was still thinking about his work.

"I think we should have dinner together. What do you say, after office, let's go to some restaurant."

Roshen thought for a moment. He had plans with Abhi to buy some stuff for his laptop. He wanted to say 'Yes' but Abhi had never cancelled his plan with Roshen. He did not even go to see Priya's exhibition when he had to do shopping for Roshen's family. But the last few days had been busy for Roshen and he wanted to spend some time with Kriti.

"What happened, a girl is asking you to have dinner with her and you are thinking. What kind of guy you are." Kriti said when Roshen was still thinking what to do.

"Ok, you decide the place and we will go there after office." Said Roshen and stood up. Kriti had not finished her tea yet but he had almost forgotten about that now.

Saying 'No' to Abhi was always a difficult task. Not because he used to get angry or sad, but he always had some argument to prove himself right. Some way or other, Abhi always managed manipulate Roshen to make him do what he wanted. But today Roshen desperately wanted to go with Kriti, not with Abhi. But he did not know how to tell Abhi that he would not go with him. In this uncertainty, he decided to lie. Just before he was leaving office, Roshen sent an sms to Abhi,

'I m busy 2day, hv a lot of work here, will cm late, can't go 2 market'

After sending the message, Roshen switched off his phone to avoid any conversation with Abhi. Roshen did not want any disturbance during dinner. *If he asks, I will tell him that the discharged battery was the so phone was switched off. Easily done.*

Dinner with Kriti went off quite well. They went to a vegetarian restaurant and had a long chat with lot of food. Girl, food and money; life is cool, the only missing thing is alcohol, Roshen thought. He missed Abhi for a moment for he was his mate whenever Roshen was drinking in last few months. After the dinner, which was quite expensive for the first time Roshen felt his pocket lighter.

When Roshen came back, Abhi's room was open, as usual, but there was no light or sound inside. *Must be drinking out in some bar today,* Roshen thought and went straight to his room. He switched on his cell phone. He had to chat again with Kriti now by text messages before sleeping, *a thing that Abhi hated a lot.*

Next morning when Roshen went office, Abhi was still sleeping. Roshen thought it would be better not to talk to him for some time, *he will soon forget.*

The day in office was again a busy one. Roshen felt he was hardly getting time for himself. It was a Saturday and he was very tired after a long week. *Yesterday I was in office, then with Kriti and now he woke up and again back in office.* He was feeling that he had been working in the office for years. Today again Kriti asked him whether he wanted to have dinner outside but Roshen refused saying that he had a headache. He wanted to take rest, have some beers with Abhi and a long conversation with him. *Seems like it's been a long time I haven't talked to him.*

"Sir, can I go home now, I have a terrible headache." Roshen asked his boss, Tiwari, when he called Roshen to ask about the progress of his work. It was about half an hour before closing time.

"Headache! Hmm..." Tiwari paused for a moment and pulled his pants upwards to the point where his tummy had the maximum diameter, then took a long breath and said,

"Take some medicine and get back to work."

"I have already taken medicine, but no use; I guess I need a doctor now." Roshen was spontaneous with his answer.

"Look at these new guys, they work for two days and start having headache." Tiwari said looking upwards as if talking to God, a habit Roshen found very irritating. Whenever he used to do that, Roshen felt like holding his face with both hands and turn it towards himself and say *'Talk to one person at a time'*. But he was silent, he wanted to leave badly.

"Look, you are already very slow and if you will leave work in between, this organization will suffer. You are new and young but still you behave this way, when I started working, I used to work more than twelve hours a day, and that also in a situation where......"

'Oh my god! His lecture will take all the remaining half hour.' Roshen thought while Tiwari started telling him one of his stories when he could not sleep for three days because of the workload.

"Sir, actually I won't get a doctor if I don't leave now." Roshen disturbed Tiwari in his story, he was now getting desperate to leave but somehow he gave Tiwari a chance to tell one more story when he was working in a village and did not get a doctor for three days when he had fever but still he did not let work suffer. *You are a superhero sir, but please let me go!*

Eventually, his story ended and Roshen was now so bored that he did not utter a word. He did not want to give Tiwari a reason to tell one more story. It was about ten minutes before the closing time and most of the people had stopped working.

"You can go now, but I want all the work done by Monday morning. Take it home or come early in the morning; I don't want any more excuses." Tawari dismissed him.

Bad move, never ask Tiwari for leave, lesson learnt!

Finally Roshen bid Kriti good bye and moved towards his apartment with some advice from Kriti to take care and of course, some files as Tiwari told him. Though he had no intensions of working on them but one thing he learnt in a few months of job experience, 'pretending to work' is more important than working itself. If you don't pretend to work hard, you are a lazy guy. If you manage to take out time for other stuff like involving in chat with co-workers or have fun in office time, then even if you are giving great output, you are always a bad employee because you don't seem to be 'involved' in your work.

When Roshen reached the apartment, Abhi was getting ready to leave and from the expression Abhi gave on seeing Roshen made Roshen realize that he probably wanted to leave before he comes. Roshen saw his wrist watch, he was about ten minutes earlier than his usual time. Abhi did not speak a word after he saw Roshen which was strange given that they had hardly seen each other in the last two days.

"Where are you going?" Roshen started first, he had a lot of things to tell Abhi, about Kriti, about Tiwari and work and he was more than disappointed to saw Abhi leaving.

"I have some work." A reply that Abhi was not interested in giving.

"I can come, if you want." Roshen made a reluctant offer. He wanted to sit a talk but roaming around with Abhi rather than sitting alone would be a far better option, he thought.

"Nah, I don't want you to come. Apparently you have a lot of 'work' these days already." Abhi said making 'sarcastic' symbol with both his hands while speaking 'work' and started walking leaving his door open as usual. Roshen did not say anything further but saw Abhi leaving quickly.

Roshen was astonished by Abhi's behavior. He had never talked to him that way. *What had happened to him?* Roshen thought a lot, maybe he is pissed off because I did not go with him yesterday. Roshen cursed his whole day. *First I refused Kriti, then Tiwari gave me a lecture and now Abhi is also behaving this way.* Roshen went into his room and sat quietly for some time. He started doing his office work while he impatiently waited for Abhi. In between he glanced out of his window a few times to see whether he was coming, but there was no sign of him. Kriti sent him few text messaged but Roshen wanted to avoid her as well so he replied that he was not feeling well and trying to sleep.

The next few hours Roshen continued to work. He went to Abhi's room in hope to find some cigarettes but he could not find any. He thought of calling Abhi but decided against it. He was feeling a little angry now. He waited till twelve and then went to sleep. *Tomorrow is Sunday, I will talk to him.*

A FIGHT BETWEEN FRIENDS

When Roshen woke up, it was eleven in the morning. He heard Abhi's footstep outside the door but was in a mood to stay in the bed for some more time. It was a cold Sunday morning and the bed was feeling far more comfortable than usual days. When he eventually got up and went to the bathroom, he caught a glimpse of Abhi smoking inside his room. *He is really upset otherwise he would have woken me up.*

Yes, Abhi was upset a lot, but not because Roshen had cancelled the plan. He was okay with Roshen cancelling the plan. In fact when he had got the message from Roshen saying that he was busy, Abhi had cancelled his program and sat down to write some story. Then he thought of surprising Roshen by going to his office. He went to a restaurant and got dinner for two people packed and took it to the Roshen's office, only to find that he left at the exact time, *with Kriti.*

After a long time, something gave Abhi a restless night, a thing that property of billions could not do. When he tried to call Roshen, his phone was off. Abhi threw the food right in front of Roshen's office on the road and came back. There were two bottles of beer in his room. He switched off all the lights and started drinking. When Roshen came back, Abhi was still drinking but he did not want to talk to Roshen. Abhi went to bed without having dinner that night thinking he would tell Roshen that they were best friends and should not lie to each other for these small things. But when Abhi woke up the next day, Roshen was already gone.

"Dude, what are you doing?" Roshen came directly into Abhi's room as he came out of bathroom and started speaking from the door.

"Nothing."

"Why didn't you wake me up? Are you upset, we haven't really talked in last couple of days." Roshen said as he walked towards Abhi.

"Actually I was busy with a story; I could not think how to end this." Abhi decided not to bring up the thing which could cause friction between them.

"Oh, can I help you?" Roshen opened a packet of cigarette and lit one.

"I have completed it. Now if you are done, let's go somewhere. I am feeling hungry. I also have to buy a new bag for my laptop." Abhi restrained himself from having an argument at the moment. A fight with Roshen was the last thing he wanted.

The day was proving to be a reunion for Abhi and Roshen. They went out and had a spicy breakfast with a tea. Abhi bought two cigars for them. Roshen was trying one for the first time and he did not really like it. Roshen was still struggling with it when Abhi took it from him and finished it. It was feeling the same way when they first met each other and used to have fun roaming in the city. The only difference was, at that time, Abhi was busier and this time, Roshen was, with his phone. He was sending messages, called Kriti three times but Abhi wasn't giving him time alone so it was never more than two-three minutes Roshen could talk to her.

After that they went to a movie, '3-idiots' which was one of the biggest hits. Roshen did not want to go in there but as it was a movie about engineering students, Abhi was more than interested to watch it, so he dragged Roshen into cinema hall, and when the movie started, Abhi was making a mess of it.

"Why aren't there any girls there in this class?" Abhi asked Roshen who was busy texting Kriti.

"That," Roshen paused and thought for a moment and said, "You should ask the director, not me." And he again got himself busy with the phone. This was Abhi's habit, He was always picking out errors in every movie he used to see and Roshen was sick of this habit.

"If this movie is a ten year old story, how come everybody has a cell phone? India was not really that much developed ten years back, was it?" Abhi once again asked Roshen who was reading some sms, Abhi this time could not bear disregard of his critical statement. He snatched Roshen's phone and started reading the message. It was from Kriti and said,

'even i m missin u, wish i were thr with u watching tht movi'

Abhi switched off Roshen's phone and gave it back to Roshen without saying anything. For the next one hour of the movie both were silent but a lot of words were dancing in their brains and both somehow stopped them from bursting out of their mouths. A nice movie somehow helped them from doing so. Whenever Abhi saw a mistake, he fought his temptation to say it. Roshen on the other hand felt that Abhi was trying to stop him from talking to Kriti. He wanted to switch his phone on but he sensed that doing this would provoke an argument with Abhi at a public place which would be a good thing to do.

After the movie was over Roshen switched on his phone and then tried to break the awkward silence between them,

"So, did you like the movie?"

"Ah, yes. It was nice."

"What do you think we should do now?"

"Whatever you say." Both were talking in as short sentences. *A sign not good for two friends.*

"I guess we should have dinner and then go back to the apartment. We can..." Roshen had not even finished when his phone started ringing.

What a pathetic situation, Abhi thought, who knew that it was Kriti. He was more than frustrated by Roshen's girlfriend. He sat down on the stairs near the gate of cinema hall and kept waiting until Roshen was finished, which took more than ten minutes.

"We are having Chinese, on MG Road there is a good restaurant." Roshen said as he came back after hanging up. Abhi did not resist, just got up and walked outside to an autorikshaw. When the day started, he was feeling like giving their friendship a new start and towards the end of the day, he realized that Kriti was far more important in Roshen's life at that point.

"So, what should we order?" Abhi asked while looking at the menu card while they both were sitting in the restaurant. He was silent for most of the time after they left the cinema hall.

"Wait, Kriti is also coming." Roshen was anxiously looking at the door of the restaurant.

"What, you invited her! And that also without telling me. What do you think I am gonna do when you two will be having dinner and talking."

"What's the problem; she said she wanted to have dinner with me so I invited her."

"Didn't you want to know whether I want to have dinner with her or not?"

"Why in the world would you have any problem?"

"Because I can't stand the two of you talking like stupid lovers with me having to listen to all that crap. It would be far better to eat alone than eating with you two." Abhi was getting louder now.

"Don't talk like that. Even I came with you when you went to meet Priya. Did you ask me then?"

"Don't you compare Priya with that bitch." Abhi stood up as he spoke those words.

"How dare you call my girlfriend a bitch?" Abhi's collar was in Roshen's hand now. Abhi was shocked the way Roshen jumped by hearing those words. For a moment he did not know what to do. He stared at Roshen for some time who kept holding his collar but now his grip was loosened. Abhi did not say anything and turned around to leave the restaurant. On his way back, he saw Kriti entering.

RANJIT'S PLAN

Sometimes we feel that we control our lives and whatever happens to us is majorly because of our actions but usually, destiny plays a big role which may be in the form of our friends who do favors that we never expect them to do and sometimes in the form of our enemies; we can never expect what plan they have for us.

Everybody has enemies and so did Abhi. But the biggest thing was, he was having an enemy in his own family, his uncle Ranjit, who, for the last few years was planning to somehow become owner of the royal property and Abhi was the only obstruction now.

"Are you prepared for the next hearing?" Ranjit asked his lawyer the third time in two days which irritated him as every time his answer was disappointing his client and this time it was no different even though he was trying his best to make a difference.

"I am working on it. Don't worry, it will be done."

"How long will it take?" Ranjit wanted the property as soon as possible though he did not realize that even if his lawyer was prepared, that would not change the date of hearing.

"The hearing is ten days from now. Why are you in such hurry?"

"What are you doing now? I have told you everything I knew about Abhimanyu. Now I want to see him not getting a penny from this property."

"I have already told you that this is not possible. He will not get any of this property only is he ceases to be." Tapan said, not trying to say things directly.

"What do you want to say?"

"Abhi has no one to take care of. If he dies, he does not have any family except you so his share would come to the last family member existing and that's you."

"So you are telling me to kill him." Ranjit had thought of this earlier but he ridiculed the idea. The guilt he had felt after pushing his elder brother to death had not disappeared and killing his only son would make him feel even worse.

"When was the last time when you talked to your nephew?" Tapan asked trying to convince Ranjit that the death of Abhimanyu at that stage would make his job much easier.

"I can't recall. I saw him at Rakesh's funeral but I don't remember talking to him. May be when he lived in the palace with us but that was a long time ago. He stole some alcohol and drank with one of his friends. Rakesh then sent him to boarding school. I have hardly seen him after that." Ranjit now realized that he was never in touch with his nephew.

"And now when your brother is no more, I don't think it matters to you whether he is alive or not until you have the property."

"Yeah, you are right."

"So if his death means that you will get his share of the property as well, which is by the way the biggest share, why shouldn't it happen?"

Ranjit Yashwardhan did not answer. After waiting a few seconds, he picked up his phone and dialed some number. *I have a man who can do it.*

PRIYA'S HOME

It is a funny thing that the higher is the age group of friends, the more time they take to resolve a conflict. A fight between two kids ends before they start to feel anything. College buddies take some time but in most of the cases, they eventually end up together. Adults take more time and efforts to make things better and sometimes, it never happens.

After Abhi left Roshen at the restaurant, Roshen could not stop thinking about what happened. He told Kriti the whole story eluding the 'bitch' part which he thought would not be appropriate to repeat. Kriti was more interested in her dinner and always wanted to finish the discussion by telling Roshen not to worry and everything would be all right, but all the time, Roshen was talking about Abhi only. *She would never understand how close they were as friends.*

When Roshen came back, he saw Abhi's room locked for the first time, a sign which expressed many things. For the next two days Abhi did not come to the apartment. Roshen was wondering where he had gone. *Would he ever come back?*

Office was going on as usual; Roshen got scolded by Tiwari for not doing his work properly, Kriti chatted with other colleagues most of the time which made Roshen jealous but there was nothing much he could do now because of the workload. Kriti did not ask Roshen for a dinner again, the last time had been too boring for her. Roshen also did not want to take her out, paying expensive bills twice made it difficult for him. *Why can't we share those bills, she earns almost as much as I do,* he wondered.

Coming back to the apartment was also difficult. It felt lonely without Abhi. Though Roshen did not want to talk to him, he expected him to be there. A locked room was something Roshen was not able to digest. New Year was approaching and kids in the building were enjoying holidays and their cacophony annoyed Roshen even more.

Abhi, on the other hand, was not having a good time either. From the restaurant, he went to Priya's house where she lived with her mother. Aunt Monika, was an independent kind of woman. She was a kind lady whose husband had abandoned her along with her two year old daughter. She spent the rest of her life waiting for him and bringing her daughter up but he never came back. However she heard a long time ago that he was living in Canada and had married a white woman there.

Abhi was, liked in their home but he did not like living there. He was used to live in a place where he got cooked food and had to live neatly, keep things in place and do everything in a proper manner. Priya was busy with work so she hardly got any time to spend with Abhi and there was hardly any communication between Aunt Monika and Abhi; she talked to Abhi only when it was necessary. There were no hard feelings but the fact that they used to meet only once in years and did not have anything in common to share along with her introvert nature were the things which stopped them from talking. Abhi respected her a lot and was always afraid of saying anything that might hurt her so he also kept his mouth shut as far as possible.

"I guess you crossed the line." Priya said when Abhi told her the whole story about him and Roshen. Aunt was cooking dinner in the kitchen and could hear almost every word spoken in the dining room, but she did not want to disturb two young people for her thoughts might be old fashioned for them. *These days, people are a lot more intelligent, or at least, they think so.*

"You also think I am wrong. You haven't seen how pathetic Roshen made his life because of that girl. It really sucks."

"Whatever, it is his personal life. You are not supposed to disturb it."

"What do you mean by personal? Am I not a part of his personal life? If a girl whom he has met just few days back is more important than me, let him think that way. I don't want to be his friend."

"So how long has it been since 'you' met Roshen?" Priya quipped.

Priya's question hit Abhi like an arrow. It had been only about six months, and yes, Roshen also met Kriti just a day after he met Abhi but to Abhi, it seemed like forever.

"It's true that you are a part of his life, but now Kriti is also a part of his life, may be bigger. You should learn to live with it." Priya continued.

Abhi did not say anything. He was still finding it difficult to accept that it was his fault. *I was the one who made things work for Roshen, how he can ignore me for her.* However he had to agree what Priya said. There was a conflict in his mind and still the part which was against Roshen, was dominating. *I cannot apologize to him, I never did anything wrong.*

"If you want, I can talk to Roshen." Priya offered.

"No, it's between me and him. I don't want any America to interrupt." Abhi refused straightaway and started having the food Aunt was serving.

Next morning, Abhi went to his apartment long after Roshen used to leave for office. Facing Roshen was the last thing he wanted to do, though he knew that it wouldn't be possible for a long time.

Abhi was feeling awkward opening the door for he had never done it before. As he entered the room, he felt that it smelled different. Abhi wondered if the room was also missing someone to smoke and drink inside. This reminded him that for the last two days, he hadn't smoked any cigarette after he left Roshen in that restaurant. There was a packet lying on the bed. Abhi, for a moment was tempted to smoke but he restrained himself for a reason he did not know. He opened his laptop and started writing a story and somehow it was not about love or affair for the first time, it was about two friends.

When Roshen came back from office, Abhi's room was bolted from inside, another thing he had never seen in the last few months. It was a clear indication from Abhi that he still did not want to talk to Roshen. *Neither do I,* Roshen thought. Though in the last few days, he had missed Abhi like never before, he still had no intentions of talking to him. *He called my girlfriend a bitch.*

The day was usual for Roshen; he went early and had a chat with Kriti for fifteen minutes, which was the longest he was getting to talk to her those days. At lunch as well, he hardly got any time which pissed off Kriti as well. Roshen's being busy was hurting their relationship and they were feeling it as well. But Roshen was still desperate to make things work and for that, he made a big decision in this premature relationship, *to propose to Kriti.*

For that, while coming back to the apartment, Roshen bought a ring and two passes for a club. The ring was one of the least expensive available as Roshen was not in a situation to buy an expensive ring. His budget was around ten thousands and he had chosen the most beautiful one he could find in that range. *It's just symbolic, I can gift her a good one later,* he thought. *Tomorrow is New Year's Eve; I will propose to her at midnight.* Everything was planned in his mind. He wanted to tell someone all this and without Abhi, there was no one he could share all this with. A bolted door also gave him a push not to talk to him. Now Roshen was anxiously waiting for New Year, may be a completely different life is waiting on the other side of 2009.

HAPPY NEW YEAR

The thing about time is, it always seems to pass slowly when we are waiting for something and when we look back in time, it feels like it moved a little too fast. One more year was about to end, and in Roshen's life, this one was very remarkable. After a struggle of more than one year, he finally got a good job; he met people and made good friends like Abhi; he was finally into a relationship and life was looking more beautiful than it ever did. There were some glitches but overall life was fascinating and the thing he decided to do on the last day, if it worked would change the whole course of his life.

Roshen woke up little late as he had found it difficult to sleep the previous night. There were so many thoughts about how he is going to do it, how Kriti would react. He realized that it was only one month since they had been together but Roshen was quite sure that Kriti was the one. *And I have to do it someday, it's better to do with a relationship in a healthy state.* Somehow the deep feeling of insecurity was also making Roshen take this step. Nevertheless, he got ready and left for office where, he knew; there wouldn't be much to do with people in a hurry to leave to join some New Year party and this time while going, he hardly noticed the closed door in the apartment.

It was a party like atmosphere in the office. Most bosses were absent and the rest were not in a mood to work. Everybody wanted it to be a holiday but the company policy did not allow it to happen. Roshen was very happy that day in spite of the fact that he was in his office on the last day of the year; this was because Tiwari was busy with some work and did not call him. With no pending work from the previous day, he got plenty of time to talk to Kriti and when he heard from some colleague that Tiwari would leave at lunch, he was ecstatic. *Lucky day,* he thought.

"I don't know what to wear tonight. What do you think, which color suits me the most?" Kriti asked Roshen amid their chat while they were sitting in the canteen.

"You look awesome dear whatever you wear. Wow! It rhymes. So it must be true."

"What do you think about pink, it is my favorite?" Kriti was not amused by the rhyme while all Roshen was thinking, was about the rhyme, *think about pink, nice!* But Kriti was more serious about her dress than a candidate in the presidential election.

"It would look gorgeous. But white would look even better. Remember the dress you were wearing last Saturday, it was great." Roshen remembered that the pink dress she had worn last time, revealed a little too much.

"Yeah, I think white would be a better choice. Anyway, did you talk to your friend after that night?"

Roshen was not expecting that question from Kriti. Kriti was never much into Roshen's personal life. Her favorite topics were movies, songs, relationships and herself. It was unsettling and he felt a surge of adrenaline rushing. It was the combination of his feelings towards Kriti and Abhi which came upon him simultaneously and he did not know how to handle them together.

"No, I did not. And I don't even want to."

The last day of any year is special occasion special for most people in many ways, but for Abhi, it was just another day. He woke up long after Roshen was gone and started to complete his story. The magazine people called him and said that they needed something really good for their January edition. *I am always good by their standards.* He also thought of seeing Mike who was asking for a meeting for more than a week but Abhi was not in a good mood to talk about property things. Priya also called him few times that morning but at that time he was fast asleep. When he woke up and tried to call her, her phone was switched off.

Abhi had not smoked in the last few days neither had he consumed any alcohol. He was feeling fresh. Till now, he used to think that he could not sleep without a drink but when he was at Priya's home, he fell asleep while talking to her. It was strange but he felt so much comfortable with her that he hardly needed any cigarette or alcohol two days when he was with Priya. He tried to continue that at his apartment as well. After a couple of hours of writing, he was ready for a nap when his phone rang. It was Priya.

"Hello"

"Come down. I am waiting."

"Where were you? I called you so many times."

"I know that. Now will you please come down? And get yourself ready, we are not coming back here today."

"What the hell are you saying?"

"Come fast. We are going my home. Mumma has cooked lunch for you."

"Okay, coming in five minutes."

Abhi sensed the urgency in her tone. *What has happened now?* He glanced out of the window; Priya was sitting in her car. *Must be in hurry, she did not even came up.*

When Abhi and Priya reached her home, Aunt Monika was waiting at the door. She welcomed them in. After Abhi settled down at the dining table, she came after him and disappeared into the kitchen. Lunch was already prepared and Aunt Monika asked Abhi whether he wanted to eat now or later. Abhi was not feeling hungry.

"I guess it would be great if we can eat it after a little while."

"Okay, as you wish." She said sitting at the table just opposite to Abhi. Priya was still in her room changing. Aunt Monica continued,

"Listen Abhi, I want to talk to you about something."

"Ya, sure." Abhi knew there was something.

"Look, I know that Priya likes you and I also know that you don't want to marry her now. But you see, she is one year older than you. The point is that I don't want her to wait for you too long then she eventually loses both; you and her youth."

"I understand that. What do you want me to do then?"

"Look, I am completely okay with you not marrying her. It is your decision. But as her friend, I want you to tell her to find some guy and marry him; because it may be too late for her to look for some suitable person a few years later. She might miss an appropriate life partner because of you." Aunt was quite straightforward and to-the-point in her conversation. Abhi was taken aback by her statements. He was just thinking of an appropriate response when Priya stepped in,

"So this was the important thing you wanted to talk about? Why can't you just let me take my own decisions?" She was certainly angry. But Aunt Monica was still calm; she was sure about what she wanted to say.

"Because I know what happens if you choose a wrong partner. I am not telling you to marry a person of my choice. I want you to marry before it is too late."

"I know what I am doing with my life. Don't drag Abhi in all this."

"What she is saying is right. You should marry someone now." Abhi spoke in between. One thing he did not know about women was that one should not intervene when two women are busy with their discussion, *they would ignore you completely.*

"I was just trying to convince Abhi." Aunt said before Abhi was finished.

"Convince what? He does not want to marry me, it's his choice. Now whether I want to or not want to marry someone else, is not his business."

"But it's my business. I am your mother and I want the best for you."

"Please don't. I can take care of myself." Said Priya and stormed out of the room slamming the door behind her. Aunt Monica wanted to say something but did not get a chance. Abhi was now silent, thinking of his lunch*; shall I ask whether I am getting it or not.*

Lunch for Roshen was a pleasant one though. Tiwari called him once and gave some work he would have to finish before afternoon of second January, the next day being a holiday. Roshen calculated that he could finish it in a couple of hours so he decided to touch it next year and enjoy the last day of this one. After that he moved to the canteen with Kriti where he was going to spend the rest of the time in office that day. Roshen decided to indulge in some net practice before playing the match of his proposal.

"When do you think you will get married?"

"I don't know. When I got this job, my parents wanted me to marry straightaway. But I told them that I will marry only when I would find the perfect guy."

"So you haven't found a perfect guy yet." Roshen was a bit disappointed by her statement.

"Look at you silly boy." Kriti pressed her hand on Roshen's. "You know what; you are the best guy I have ever met. You are winning this race by miles."

What does she thinks I am, a horse? Who gives a damn, I am winning. Roshen stopped talking and started concentrating on the speech he was going to give while proposing Kriti. He was dreaming about the time when he would propose to Kriti, he hoped she would jump at hearing his proposal and then they both would kiss again at midnight.

Things were not very cool at Priya's home. Though Abhi got his lunch, he was abandoned by the two women. None of them was talking to him. Priya locked herself in her room and Aunt Monica got herself busy in some other work. It felt quite awkward to eat alone in some other person's home even though he was not being considered a guest as such. After eating, Abhi started listening music on his mobile phone but he was very self-conscious about it. He did not want Aunt Monika to feel that he was enjoying himself when she had just had a fight with her daughter.

After about two hours, Priya came out and went to the bathroom across the hall. Abhi thought that she had been crying inside her room but when she came back, she was looking absolutely normal.

"Did you have lunch?"

"Yes" the word came out very slowly. Abhi coughed and said, "You haven't eaten anything. Why don't you have something?"

"No, we are going out."

"But..." Abhi's sentence was cut short by Aunt Monica,

"You are going nowhere until you eat. Have lunch and then do whatever you want." There was a command in her voice and Priya did not protest. She silently had her lunch while Abhi realized he had to wait one more hour so he sat on the sofa and soon fell asleep.

Abhi did not wake up for the next few hours. He remembered Priya waking him up and guiding him to the bed but he was feeling so sleepy he did not even wonder that she was telling him to go out before having lunch. When he woke up, Priya was not there. Aunt Monica told Abhi that she had gone to some friend's home and would come soon. She also said that Priya wanted to have dinner outside with him so he had to stay and wait for her till she came. There was a silence again between Aunt and Abhi. He was now missing being with Roshen. *He was always good company.*

Soon Priya came back when Abhi was listening to some music on his phone, a thing he did only when he was very bored. Priya helped only a little to cheer him up. She herself was in a bad mood and this was probably the worst New Year's Eve Abhi had ever had though he had not remember what he did on the earlier ones. Abhi did not say anything until Priya herself told him that they were going to have dinner. Soon they were sitting in a restaurant with roasted chicken on their table. Abhi, after trying several times to talk, had given up and was having a boring dinner.

"Why can't you marry me?" Priya asked a question which almost gave Abhi a panic attack. He felt that the chicken he was about to shove in his mouth, was laughing at him.

"What are you saying?" Abhi answered with another question.

"I am asking what is wrong with you. I am tired of rejecting proposals daily. Mamma wants me to marry and you don't want to marry me. What am I supposed to do?"

"Look, you are a wonderful girl. Anybody would be lucky to marry a girl like you."

"Then why not you?"

"I don't know. I like you a lot but I cannot marry you. I cannot marry anyone. It is just not my thing."

"Wow, what an explanation, 'not my thing'. I guess I am the only idiot on this earth who is waiting for a person who does not want to marry me because it is not his 'thing'."

Priya was clearly angry with Abhi's attitude. Abhi did not answer. He just kept eating and was deep in his thoughts. There was a long silence between them. They finished their dinner and Priya paid the bill while Abhi waited for her outside. He had spent all his money already this month and Priya knew that. She dropped him at his apartment long before midnight. She knew that if they both stayed together till midnight, it would make their New Year's Eve even worse. When Priya stopped the car outside the building, Abhi said before opening the door.

"Marry someone Priya; don't waste your life for someone like me."

Abhi opened the door, stepped outside and slammed it back when Priya called him,

"Abhi"

"Yes?" Abhi knelt down to face her.

"I will wait for you."

Abhi did not speak further. Priya changed the gears and drove away quickly.

When Abhi reached the apartment, Roshen was having a great time with Kriti in a night club. After office was over, Kriti went to her home and Roshen came to the apartment. To his surprise, Abhi was not there but his door was open. Roshen changed quickly, picked the ring up and went to pick Kriti up. They both had some junk food at the stalls outside the city mall and then headed to the club. All the time Roshen was rehearsing the dialogues he wanted to speak at midnight to propose to her. Kriti was wearing a white dress which Roshen thought was an indication of how much she liked him. It was ten when they reached the club which was noisier than Roshen thought it would be.

People were dancing, shouting and drinking. When they both entered, Roshen felt a bit uncomfortable. It was not the place where he wanted to start a new life. Also with this much noise Roshen felt that it was going to be difficult to propose to Kriti because they could hardly hear anything except loud music and occasional shouts from the crowd.

Kriti did not have any problem in getting used to the noise. She started dancing soon after entering inside. Roshen was feeling awkward there but he preferred not to leave Kriti alone so he joined her as well but soon he was tired of dancing so he dragged Kriti to the bar.

Every drink in the bar was more expensive than usual but Roshen wanted to sit and talk. However talk was not really possible there. He had beer while Kriti ordered vodka. For a moment Roshen felt something. He always knew that Kriti drank and he had no problem with that but now when he was going to propose to, he was thinking what his parents would think if they know that he was marrying a girl who wore revealing dresses and drank. But this was no time to think

Soon it was just half an hour away from midnight and the club was more than full. There was hardly any space to dance. Roshen was still sitting while Kriti came back to him after dancing a little. Every sentence they were trying to speak was taking a lot of efforts so they preferred not to talk and enjoy the party. When Roshen was staring at one of the girls, Kriti slowly slapped his head.

"What?" Roshen shouted. Kriti pointed towards his phone and shouted,

"Going to talk. Coming in two minutes."

"Ok, come soon."

Kriti did not wait to listen and went outside. Roshen again went busy in ogling some chick deempy clothes. It was the only source of entertainment for him there. While Kriti was taking her time, he took one more beer and was a little drunk now. There was one girl who seemed like the one he had proposed to in his college days. He looked at his watch, it was less than ten minutes before midnight and Kriti was nowhere. *How long she will take to finish this call?* It was the time Roshen wanted to propose to her and give her that ring. *Just before midnight*, as it was planned.

Roshen took his phone out and called her, but all the networks were jammed. He was feeling a bit concerned now. He looked here and there but there was no sign of her. He tried her phone again with the same result. In desperation, he came outside and started looking for her on the road. It was now five minutes before midnight and he was losing hope. *One more time,* he thought and called on her phone again. He was now feeling that someone in heavens did not want him to be happy. He was standing on the road now.

It was less than a minute now and Roshen sat down on a stone on the footpath. He could hear the sounds of people shouting countdowns. Roshen felt helpless. The moment he thought would be a wonderful one, turned out to be the most depressing one. As the clock ticked to midnight, he saw a couple kissing each other across the road. They were looking complete with each other and this made Roshen miss Kriti even more. A few seconds later, the couple started walking towards Roshen. They both were wearing white dresses. Roshen looked at his phone; the call was still not connecting. Then he looked at that couple. He tried to have a close look at them, one figure was looking familiar. As they came closer, Roshen's jaw dropped and heartbeat rose. He now recognized the girl.

She was Kriti.

PROPERTY SEALED

The New Year started in the worst possible way for Roshen. He saw Kriti kissing some other guy. He was shattered. Kriti also saw him and did not try to avoid him. She came to Roshen and told that the guy with him, Rachit, was her old boyfriend, she had broken up with some time back. She tried to explain to Roshen that she really loved Rachit and could never love him in the same way. Roshen was barely listening to her while she was telling him that she still wants to be friends with him. For Roshen, the worst nightmare came true and now he was being asked to be part of it. The first relationship of his life ended in betrayal.

Roshen spent the first day of January in bed. There were lots of things in his mind. He could not sleep all night. Initially he was very angry. He was thinking of hitting Kriti, yelling at her, but as time passed, he started thinking about how much time he had wasted because of Kriti, how much money he had spent, he even had a fight with his best friend. After that he started missing being with Kriti, he was recalling her kisses, how she used to talk and comfort him whenever he was in distress. These thoughts made him feel terrible and he felt he was having a problem in breathing in the morning air. By the time it was seven in the morning, he fell asleep.

Abhi smoked for the first time in the last few days. What had happened the previous day had completely disturbed his thought process. Till now, he always hated the idea of marriage and events at Priya's home, made him hate it even more. *Why is marriage so important when we can stay happy without it?* He also realized that Roshen was in the apartment whole day but he tried not to think about him, though it was not easy.

But the events of the previous day were not all that Abhi was worried about. Along with problems in his social life, he was having financial problem as well. As a routine, every month a handsome amount of money was transferred into Abhi's account from his family funds. Abhi had not got any money this month which worried Abhi a little though he was quite sure that he would not have to face money problems. *It must be in my account by now,* Abhi thought and set to go to the nearest ATM to check whether money was transferred or not, but to his surprise, there was still no money in his account.

Though Abhi did not have cash in his account, he still had some in his pocket. All the notes in his pocket were leftovers from purchasing cigarettes and having tea outside but for the moment, they were sufficient to buy him a breakfast but yet, money was a problem now as money in his pocket would not suffice even for two days; a problem Abhi was facing the first time in his life.

All his life, Abhi had lent money to friends, acquaintances and paid for random people who never gave it back but now when he was feeling he was out of money, he did not know whom to ask. He had to buy stuff to upgrade his laptop, to drink and many other things. He thought of borrowing from Priya but his ego came in between, asking for money was not acceptable to him. So he headed towards the alternate source of money, the magazine office.

For all these years, whenever Abhi got payment for a story, he got a cheque in the name of the orphanage to donate it but for the first time, he wanted the payment for himself. *I will make the donation when money comes in my account.* He was still wondering why he did not get money this month. For last so many years, it had been coming before the month started without a mistake. Even when his father died, the process was not disturbed. *I should wait for some time, the money will definitely come.*

The owner of the magazine was a generous person, Mr. Rohit Pancholi. He was forty and had left his job as a reporter with a news channel to set up his own magazine. He always liked Abhi and his stories. Abhi was a welcomed guest in his office.

"Wow, you came so early this month. I needed your story before tenth of this month." Said Mr. Pancholi with a smile when Abhi entered Abhi never came before or after the date he was asked to come and he never came without a story.

"Yeah, but I needed to give you this story today." Abhi said Sitting on the chair in front of him.

"What happened?"

"Nothing, I just want payment a little early."

"That's not a problem. You could have asked for it without giving your story. You know, we are adding some new contents in our mid January edition. I want this edition to be very good so I really want a nice story."

"This is so far my best story. I am sure you would love it."

"I always do. Give me you pendrive. I can't wait to read it." Mr. Pancholi took out his cheque book to pay Abhi.

"One more thing Rohit, can you pay me cash this time?"

"Not a problem." he said putting his cheque book back in his drawer. Then he called someone on his office phone and while talking, inserted the pen drive in his desktop.

"Just wait for five minutes." He told Abhi after he hung up and got busy in reading the story while Abhi waited silently. In less than five minutes, a peon came with an envelope in his hand for Abhi. Rohit preferred giving it to Abhi with his own hands so leaned forward to take the envelope from peon's hands and gave it to Abhi.

"These are seven thousand. Five for your story and two you can say New Year's bonus. Actually your stories are too good to be sold for only five grands."

"Thank you Rohit. Call me when you need another one." Abhi said standing from his chair.

"Wait a minute Abhi. I want to say something to you."

"Yeah," Abhi did not sit, an indication to Rohit to make it fast. I got my money; my work here is done; now I have to move.

"Listen, we are starting a new educational magazine. I want you to work as an editor. I know you don't want a permanent job but I want you to think over it. You deserve more than two stories a month."

"Ok, I will let you know. Anyways, thanks for this." Abhi said waving his envelope and left the office briskly.

Having money in his hand, Abhi felt like he had got some oxygen for few more days. He knew that it was not going to last long enough and he needed his real source back in position, so as he came out of the magazine office, he took his cell phone out, searched for the name, Mike, and dialed.

"Where have you been for so long?" was Mukesh's first words while answering the phone call. He had left several messages on Abhi's phone when he was not answering but it was the first time Abhi got in touch with him in last few days.

"I was a little busy. What happened?"

"I need your signatures on some legal documents. I was trying to call you but you never answered. I even went to your apartment but you weren't there either."

"Ya, don't worry, we can meet today. Listen, I want you to do one more thing."

"What is that?"

"I did not get my money this month. I want you to talk Mr. Bhati about this. He takes care of all the finances."

"Abhi, I am afraid this won't be possible for him either."

"Why?"

"Court ordered to seal the royal property until this case is solved."

PARTY IN OFFICE

Roshen was finding it more difficult to face the break up than he ever imagined. He locked himself in his room. Tears started flowing from his eyes when he woke the up next day. He somehow managed to go out for breakfast but his thoughts were kept coming back to the events that happened last night. When he was eating, he was oblivious to the taste of food. He tried to smoke to suppress his frustration but it didn't help either. He sent some sentimental messages to Kriti but there was no response. He resisted for some time and then called her only to hear the reliance music he used to hear every time he called her but this time it was very irritating.

The next day Roshen reached office at his usual time, half an hour early. He desperately wanted to talk to Kriti; he thought perhaps if he would beg her to come back to him she would. He was ready to do anything to be with Kriti and this made his condition really terrible and in the absence of Abhi, there was no one to console or guide him. The first break up of his life was really making him behave illogically.

Kriti did not come at the time she used to. When she came; she was with her boyfriend who did not leave until Roshen saw him with Kriti. *One more slap in Roshen's face, but he did not really want to understand this.*

"What happened to you, you are looking very dull do you have fever?" one of the colleagues asked Roshen who could not stop staring at Kriti.

"Nothing, just a little headache."

Roshen chose to concentrate on his work. The job Tiwari gave him to finish before lunch was taking more time majorly because of his thoughts which were still lingering in the past. Every time he tried to think about work, it was Kriti's thought which came and haunt him and in few cases, it was her voice or a sight. He now realized that even if he tried to forget her, it was going to be very difficult as he had to work with her. *Abhi was right, having affair with a girl in office was a very bad idea.*

"I hope you have completed the job I gave to you." Tiwari called Roshen and asked. From the smell coming out of Tiwari's mouth, it was evident that he had just smoked a cigarette. When Roshen imagined him smoking a cigarette in his unique attire, he found it funny even a bad mood*; Holding his pants with one hand and cigarette in other.*

"Sir, I will complete it in one hour and give it to you before lunch is over."

"Oh, so my lazy boy is going to work in lunch time as well. Then you must not be coming in tonight's party as well. You would like to work even then also."

"What party sir? I don't know about any party."

"That means you haven't got the invitation yet. Don't worry; it will reach your table. The company is throwing a party. We got a new project in Qatar and it's New Year as well. So you better finish your work fast. And take lunch, but don't waste much time."Tiwari was apparently in a good mood today. *Everybody is happy except me*, thought Roshen. While going back to his desk, he kept staring at Kriti. She was busy gossiping with Neha. She also noticed that Roshen was looking at her all the time, and this time in a different way. She decided to ignore him as much as possible, *as per the prescription of her 'new boyfriend'*.

That day, office ended one hour earlier to give everybody enough time to get ready for the party. Roshen tried to have a chat with Kriti but she knew that Roshen would try it and did not want to give him a chance to talk. Rachit was waiting for her outside. After signing the register, she moved quickly towards the exit where Roshen was already waiting for her at the door.

"Kriti, listen to me." Roshen said as Kriti was passing him. Roshen did not realize that somebody else was keeping an eye on him.

"What is your problem dude?" Rachit came from nowhere and stood in front of Roshen.

"Look, I want to talk to Kriti." Roshen tried to move forward towards Kriti but was stopped before he could do anything.

"She does not want to talk to you. And if you want to stay safe, keep away from her." There was a clear warning in those words which did not bother Roshen at all but few persons of his office were now looking at him. Roshen knew that was not the place where he could possibly talk to her.

"Let him go Rachit. Talking to such people won't serve any purpose." Kriti said while she started walking towards Rachit's bike parked a few feet away. Rachit left Roshen and walked towards Kriti. Both got on to the bike and disappeared.

Kriti was gone but what she had said hurt Roshen very bad. He was feeling insulted in front of his colleagues and at the same time very angry with Kriti. *Two days back, she loved me and now she calls me 'such people'.* Soon people looking at him went away but Roshen was left fuming. *First she cheats on me and then insults me in front of everyone; Abhi was right; she is a bitch.*

Roshen was in confused about whether to go to the party or not. If he did not go, he will have to stay at the apartment alone where numerous thoughts would haunt him again and if he went, he would have to face Kriti. But he knew that avoiding Kriti could not be an option as he had to face her daily in the office anyways, if he went there, he would get free liquor and dinner plus if he got a chance, he can give it back to Kriti.

The party was in an enormous garden where on one side there were drinks of various varieties including many kinds of cocktails. On the other side, there was food which was also divided in two different sections of vegetarian and nonveg. On the left side there were stalls of fast food which lured most of the females. Roshen saw Kriti standing with Neha and Sangeet on a far corner. He preferred to stay away from them.

The person Roshen talked most in his office after Kriti and Sangeet was Tiwari. He was always a guy who never indulged himself in group conversations and gossips. Sangeet, his old friend was also not talking to him after that fake birthday party and with Kriti, Roshen had never felt the need to talk to anyone but now in the party, he was searching for company. There were a few groups, he joined but he found them very boring. He saw Tiwari drinking with few higher officials and wished him but he did not want to talk to him either. So he found a chair in one corner and started drinking.

One and half hour and Roshen was drinking continuously without realizing that he was drinking too much to handle. Continuous drinking with Abhi for such a long time had increased his capacity to drink but this time the events that had happened in last few days combined with alcohol shattered his mental balance. Images in front of his eyes were getting blurred each passing minute. He saw Kriti having her dinner with someone in a corner and could not hold himself this time. *I want to talk to her and no one can stop me from doing that.*

Roshen stood up and started staggering towards her without realizing that in the way he almost hit Tiwari who noticed that Roshen was certainly sloshed and don't know what he was doing. There was a need to control him and as his boss, he was going to fulfill this duty.

"What do you mean by 'such people'?" Roshen approached Kriti and pulled her arm. Her boyfriend was not there this time Roshen noticed that.

"Excuse me; I don't want to talk to you." Kriti was very polite. She knew that Roshen was drawing everybody's attention.

"Wow, you are really a bitch. First you cheat on me and then you insult me. You think I am the biggest asshole in the world who would let you do anything you want."

"I should go now." Kriti started to move. The 'Bitch' word suddenly attracted a lot of people and they were enjoying the scene

Kriti did not want to be a part of.

"Why, you are feeling ashamed now. You did not felt that when you kissed someone on the road when you were supposed to be with me." Roshen was now a lot louder.

"Roshen!" A solid voice diverted everybody's attention. It was Tiwari who was silent till now.

"Mind your language; you don't know how to talk to ladies." He was shouting at Roshen. But Roshen was not listening; he was not yet done with Kriti.

"You won't go anywhere. I need to talk to you and I will." Roshen moved towards Kriti who was trying to hide behind Tiwari now. Tiwari stopped him in between.

"Roshen, if you will speak one more word, you are fired."

"Look who is talking. I don't want to take orders from someone who doesn't know how to wear pants." There was a silence after Roshen said this sentence. Everybody realized Roshen was in trouble now.

"Do you know what are you saying? I am your boss." Tiwari was trying to gather some confidence which was shaken by that statement. He never thought Roshen could say those words and in a sober condition, perhaps even Roshen could not think that.

"Yes, you are a boss everyone hates. If some day I become your boss, I would so like you to slap your face." Roshen said those words when he was struggling to stand straight and, needless to say, everybody listening was enjoying the entertainment.

"Oh, you can do whatever you want because you don't work with me anymore. You are fired already." Tiwari was standing tall in front of Roshen as if inviting him to slap.

There were incidences in Roshen's life when he wanted to slap people. He wanted to slap every interviewer who did not select him, he wanted to slap Abhi when he called Kriti a bitch, he wanted to slap both Kriti and Rachit after he saw them kissing but never in his life he wanted to slap Tiwari except this one moment. The difference between all those moments and this one moment was that, he was really drunk now and a person he hated was almost offering him to slap. He lunged forward and with all his power, which was very little that time by the way, slapped his boss.

DAY AFTER THE PARTY

Life is like a game which changes rules in between to adjust its result. One moment, you feel that you are winning this game and next moment, the person winning turns out to be the biggest loser. Roshen was definitely winning this game just few days back but in last few days since he started losing, he lost his friend first, then a girlfriend and now....

Next morning when Roshen wake up, he felt like he had had a horrible dream. Then he noticed that his cloths were torn at places and his mouth smelled very bad. When he moved on his bed, he felt some pain in his joints and by the time he was completely awake, scenes from last night were dancing in front of his eyes and thinking of them, his heart was sinking.

That slap on Tiwari's face was a start. Tiwari felt so much insulted by the slap that he held Roshen's collar and started abusing him. Roshen was very much ready to get into a fight and a small fight took place between them which was soon resolved by other persons and then Roshen was thrown out of the party. Roshen did not remember what happened to Kriti. *Perhaps she left before all that happened.* He also did not know what Tiwari said but he knew one thing, he had screwed both, his love life and his career in just two days, *the first two days of a new year.*

After he remembered everything, Roshen's head started aching. Suddenly his room appeared a lot smaller to him. He stood up and opened the window. It was a cloudy day outside. He looked at his mobile, it was showing eleven in the morning but yet there was no sunshine. Just two days back, he would have said that it was very romantic and perfect for a picnic but now he wanted sunshine which was nowhere.

Roshen left his bed and went to bathroom. Abhi's room was open now but he was not there. Roshen splashed water in his face and looked himself in mirror. It was a strange feeling as he was looking at a person he did not know. He was looking at a person who had ruined everything he had, friend, girlfriend and now… job. *How would I tell my family?* It was a scary thought. Though there was not much responsibility on his shoulders at that time but the family banked highly on him for money for her sister's marriage. *They were planning to buy a car. What would happen to that dream now?*

Should I beg Tiwari to save my job, they may haven't fired me yet? It was a long shot that Roshen was not fired yet because the first thing Tiwari did that morning after coming to the office was to write an application to HR department about his behavior last night and told other higher officials to make sure that Roshen was out of the company. Roshen realized that his behavior was too bad to be forgiven and he knew that because of what he had said to Tiwari, he would try to sue him even after he was fired from his job.

When Roshen came out of the bathroom, there was an emptiness surrounding him. *What next?* It was a big question. He did not want to go home and tell everyone that suddenly he was jobless now. Neither did he want to stay in at this apartment where he did not have anything to do now.

Roshen started calculating in his mind a way to reach home. I do not have a train ticket and it would take more than two weeks to get it. If I go by bus, I will have to change several times, with this much luggage that won't be possible. By plane it would be too expensive. The thought of an air ticket made him think of Abhi who had given him a ticket home and then every little thing Abhi had done for him from the day he came in the city was coming in his thoughts. *We were great together.* He knew that the thing he would miss most about this life was the time he spent with Abhi. He decided he needed to do some repair work before he even thought of leaving.

Talking to Abhi did not seem very difficult after Roshen decided to do it. He did not know how he would start talking to Abhi. Unlike all other times, he did not prepare a speech. He just wanted to speak his heart out in front of Abhi. He wanted to tell him that he would always regret that fight in the restaurant. Roshen stood up and went to Abhi's room. He did not want to talk to him on phone. He wanted to hug him when he was saying sorry so he decided to wait for him in his room only.

Roshen went to Abhi's room after a span of several days and it was looking a bit different. Though the amount of mess was the same, the smell was a little different than it used to be. Abhi's laptop was not on the floor; it was switched off and kept on the table instead which was a rare sight. There were no cigarette butts on the floor this time and the small fridge did not have beers in it. Abhi's room was suspiciously clean. One packet of cigarette was lying on the bed. Roshen needed it. *I am going to say sorry to Abhi, I guess I can use it.*

Roshen lit the cigarette and started smoking. He felt a little reluctant to flick the ash on the clean floor, was a strange thing in Abhi's room. He saw an ashtray which was hardly used. It was a circular tray with a silver outline and a golden bottom layer. Roshen took it and placed it on the table and tried to relax on the chair.

With turmoil inside and cigarette in hand, Roshen was waiting for Abhi. After a major part of the cigarette was over Roshen suddenly noticed that something was written at the bottom of the ashtray. He looked at it closely, and then he touched it. The bottom was moving; it was perhaps a golden coin, a big gold coin.

Roshen took it out of the tray and cleaned the ash on it. He looked at it closely, it was not a coin. It was a medal, a gold medal Abhi had won in his college days. *Idiot, he does not have any respect for his achievements.* A gold medal was something Roshen had always dreamed of. He saw his classmates receiving it at the convocation, he saw it in the drawing room of some of his relatives but he never received one. Today he had one in his hand and the person it belonged to, did not think of it as anything more than ash. Roshen thought something and put it in his shirt pocket. He did not have any intensions of stealing it from Abhi; he just wanted to feel it for some time.

More than half an hour passed but Abhi did not come. Roshen lit his fifth cigarette. He was so occupied with his thoughts that he did not feel that time was passing so quickly. He was just lighting cigarettes one after another and thinking about the events that had happened in last few days and his future after all this mess when he heard footsteps outside the apartment. He wished it were Abhi but the sound was not a familiar one, neither was the person who was standing at the door after a few seconds.

It was a tall and bulky man with a mustache, wearing a Kurta and a golden chain; it looked like a traditional dress. He had a few scars on his face. At first sight, the person looked quite intimidating. Roshen was standing across the room smoking. For a moment, he forgot that the person on the door is an outsider.

"Are you Abhimanyu?" the person asked in a husky voice.

"Who are you?" Roshen was nervous. The intent of the man was clearly not to have a conversation. He appeared like a burglar to Roshen.

The man did not answer. He took Roshen's response to his question to be affirmative. Both hands came out of his pocket with something. It was not clear to Roshen what it was but he figured out that he was trying to make some connection between the objects. After a few seconds, when he realized what it was, his blood curdled.

The man was pointing a gun at Roshen and he did not know what to do. He had seen guns in movies, He was experiencing for the first time how it felt to have one. His hands automatically rose upwards but the man clearly had no intentions of making him surrender. Without wasting any time, he fired the first shot. It hit Roshen in his stomach. Roshen felt that part of his body went numb for some time. He put a hand there and it was full of blood. Soon it was a pain Roshen could not bear. He cried loudly but the man was already gone, and before he left, he fired two more shots at Roshen, *just to make sure.*

HOSPITAL

It is said, in the last moments of life, a man remembers the person he loves the most. For Roshen, there was no particular person but there were images from his past that revolved around him, his family, old friends, Kriti and Tiwari, his apartment and then, Abhi. The excruciating pain was killing Roshen and he was feeling it difficult even to cry. But suddenly he knew that he did not need to cry. Soon he found that there were hands helping him to move and those hands were familiar. It was Abhi.

It was a pure coincidence that Abhi had come there at that time. When he left the apartment, he wanted to spend one more day at Priya's home but when Priya told him that she would be busy all day, Abhi decided that he could not spend whole day with Aunt Monika staying silent with a big turmoil his mind. He told Priya to drop him at his apartment. He never thought he would find Roshen at the apartment and that also in his room with blood all over his body.

"What happened to you?" Abhi screamed as he started to understand the situation but Roshen could not hear. His pain was killing his senses. Though Abhi was not alien to such panic situations, this was so far the worst he had faced. He knew he would need help and help was near. *Priya would not be too far by this time.*

A few moments later, Roshen felt himself raised up and moving towards the door. He was still bleeding and there was no first aid available in the apartment. Abhi was racing down the stairs carrying Roshen. All his power was being tested at that time and Abhi sure had no intentions of giving up easily. It was strange, how in desperate conditions, a skinny Abhi was carrying Roshen, who was at least more than one and half times his weight.

Soon Abhi put Roshen in the car and it was racing towards the nearest hospital. His heart was pounding loudly; he was hardly able to think. Priya asked him several times what had happened but he did not answer. He was looking at Roshen's face which had a few stains of blood. Tears started to flow from Abhi's eyes, a thing that had not happened ever at the death of his father.

"What happened actually?" Priya asked Abhi after Roshen was admitted in the intensive care unit and an FIR was lodged by Abhi in the police station nearby. Roshen was being operated inside and Abhi and Priya were sitting in the corridor.

"I have no idea... When I went to my room, Roshen was lying on the floor... I did not know what to do, so I called you." Abhi was speaking more slowly than usual. There was still a lot of blood on his clothes.

"He was in your room; I thought you two were not talking to each other. Then what was he doing in your room?"

"I don't know. He should have been in his office at this time. He never takes leave. There must be something very wrong."

"Should we tell his family?"

"I don't think so. First of all they can't cure him and till we don't know what happened, I don't think it would be a good idea to call them."

"Don't you think they have a right to know what is going on in Roshen's life? And if something goes wrong inside, don't they have the right to see him for the last time?"

"Look, it will take them at least a day to reach here. So we better see how Roshen is doing. I am sure nothing would go wrong. I know Roshen, he is a survivor." Abhi said and then a long silence followed.

More than two hours passed. Priya called her mom and told her about the incident. She offered to come but Priya told her not to. One policeman came meanwhile and asked about Roshen's condition. He was still unconscious. Abhi prayed to God sitting there, *one more thing he had not done in a long time*. Various thoughts were crossing his mind when a doctor came out to talk to him.

"How is he now?" Priya stood up and asked. Abhi was staring at the doctor.

"Still not conscious, but don't worry, he would be fine."

Abhi jumped up from his seat. The statement from the doctor suddenly gave him a lot of energy. He did not know much about Roshen's chances of surviving but looking at the blood over his body and thought of gunshots in his body made him think of something fatal.

"A very lucky escape," Doctor said, "He got one shot in his lower abdomen and one on his shoulder. I guess there was a third one also which almost got through this but could not reach him." Doctor said handling over a gold medal to Abhi. Abhi took it and looked at it closely. It had a tiny hole at almost the centre and the metal nearby was melted and turned black. Abhi recognized that it was his gold medal he had won in sports in college days.

"Had this thing not been there, it could have been difficult to save him." Doctor continued. Abhi was feeling proud holding the medal, as if he had just won it.

"By the way, the next time you bring someone injured, make sure that you try to stop the bleeding first."

Abhi bowed his head and started scratching it like a kid. Priya asked whether they could see Roshen now. Doctor permitted them but warned them not to disturb him. They went inside, Roshen was sleeping. Abhi looked at his face and felt the happiness he didn't know how to express. He knew that when Roshen would wake up, there won't be any dispute between them. They would always remain best friends. He looked at Priya and said,

"I told you, he is a survivor."

ROSHEN WAKES UP

It took almost twenty-four hours before Roshen could actually talk. He was lying on the hospital bed all the time and Abhi chose not to leave him until he was absolutely fine and whenever he had to go somewhere, Priya was always there to take his place. He had gained consciousness a few times earlier but was too weak even to move. When he was finally in a condition to talk, he saw both Priya and Abhi sitting in the same room. Priya was reading some book and Abhi was dozing on a chair. Priya saw Roshen opening his eyes. She put her hand on Roshen's forehead and asked,

"How are you feeling now?"

"Fine. Who brought me here, Abhi?" Roshen tried to move his head to have a look at his body which was strapped up at the wounded places. It was painful as he had been lying in the same position for so long.

"Yes" Priya said. Abhi was now awake. For a moment he hesitated but then he stood up and went to Roshen to talk. *Someone had to start it.*

"How are you doing?" asked Abhi as if he was meeting an acquaintance after a long time.

"Awesome, just been fired, both by a gun and from my job."

Roshen tried to crack a joke but Abhi did not find it funny when he heard that Roshen had been fired from his job. He knew how important that job was for Roshen. Roshen then started telling him the whole story about what had happened in last few days, how he had broken up with Kriti and slapped Tiwari after getting drunk and how he was shot by a stranger in Abhi's room. Though he narrated shorter version of everything, Abhi was full of questions and a tired Roshen was finding it difficult to answer all them but at the same time, it was feeling great sharing everything with Abhi once again, and once they started, they almost forgot that Priya was also sitting there.

"Wow, you slapped that jerk Tiwari, bravo man, he deserved it. But it would have been more fun if you had slapped Kriti instead. She turned out to be a real bitch."

"I would like to slap her one day, and her boyfriend as well. They insulted me in front of lot of people."

"I bet you would. But why did you not slap her that night?"

"I was shocked. She came to me and started saying that she missed Rachit all the time she was with me and they were meant for each other and such crap. Plus her boyfriend looked like a strong person. I did not want to lose a girlfriend and then got beaten up at midnight."

"Oh, and instead you lost a girlfriend, slapped your boss, got fired and got beaten by a bunch of people in your office party, of course much better option, isn't it."

"Don't tell me how badly I screwed up dude. I don't know how to tell my parents all this. They will be shocked. Anyways, did you tell them about my being admitted to hospital?"

"Not yet. Do you want me to tell them?"

"Hell no. Do I have fewer surprises in stock for them already? It would kill them." Roshen was very spontaneous which made Abhi a little proud on his decision not to call his parents. He looked at Priya as he was trying to say, *look, I was right.*

"So, who do you think was the person who tried to kill you?" Priya asked after staying silent for a while.

"I have no clue at all. I saw him for the first time in my life."

"That means somebody sent him to kill you." Abhi said trying to think whether all this was making a sense at all.

"Not me, somebody sent him to kill you."

Abhi was stunned to hear that. *Why would somebody want to kill me, when on the earth have I tried to wrong someone?* He wanted to ask so many questions but before he could, their discussion was interrupted by a knock on the open door. It was a police constable who came to take the statement of Roshen. He asked everybody to vacate the room. Abhi moved out along with Priya who, while going, waved towards Roshen saying that she would now come in the evening. She was already being left out in the conversation of Abhi and Roshen, though she found story of Roshen quite funny; but she had her own paintings to finish as well.

Abhi came out to see off Priya. She was a great help all the time. She refused to leave Abhi alone at the hospital. She brought food for him and sat with Roshen whenever Abhi went somewhere. All night she was awake and Abhi knew, all that was not for Roshen. At night, Priya wake him up and then they both had dinner, Priya had got packed food from home, sitting in the hospital canteen. Abhi felt it was better than any expensive dinner in a five star. They were both sitting together and talking about their childhood when they used to play games together at Priya's home. Abhi was always chased and beaten by his friends and then Priya used to tell him stories to divert his attention and make him stop crying. Priya used to come to Abhi's home to watch TV and Abhi was always disturbing her because he wanted to play games. Then Abhi went to boarding school and everything changed. There were no means of communication and Abhi got so involved in his new life that he almost forgot Priya. Even when Priya once came to meet him with her mom, he hardly had any time to spend with her.

When Abhi got admission in engineering, Priya was also doing her graduation in Mumbai. They started seeing each other again. Abhi always used to make fun of art Priya chose to make her career in but Priya was always determined to become an artist. She used to make paintings and show them to Abhi who was always critical about them. Then one day, Priya told Abhi that she loved him and would like to marry him some day. But Abhi always had a strong opinion about marriages. He did not want to marry all his life. After some time, Priya left the city and came back to live with her mom. Abhi was also destined to come back and after that he decided he not to take up a job, Priya helped him in finding an apartment in the same town nearby which was now more than a home to Abhi.

"Thank you Priya." Abhi said those awkward words he wanted to say when they both stepped out of the hospital. There was a different kind of smell outside, Abhi felt since he had been inside for long. The day was cloudy and Priya was looking a lot more beautiful than usual.

"You know there is no need to say that. Roshen is my friend as well."

"Not for him, thanks for being with me, all the time."

"I am always with you." Priya smiled and started walking towards the car parking area half expecting Abhi to follow. Abhi wanted to walk with her some more time, but it was one of the occasion when people find it awkward doing things they have been doing all their life, without knowing that they are meant to do it that way, always.

ABHI'S STORY

Several days in the hospital gave Roshen a lot of time to introspect. All his life, he was busy in preparing for some exam, interview, looking for jobs and when he finally got a job, he was so involved in his new life that he hardly had any time to think about himself. Now, he did not have anything but a friend. Though Abhi was with him for most parts of the day but there were several hours daily when Roshen was completely alone in his room. So he was in a way, forced to think all that time.

Roshen's room was not a big one yet it was a quite comfortable for one person to stay. Besides a bed, there were two chairs and the rest of the room was empty. It felt very nice to stay in a clean room after a long time. *A person, who lives in that apartment, would find most of the rooms in this world, clean.* Roshen was quite sure that Abhi was paying a good amount to get him treated in this hospital, *typical of Abhi.*

After Roshen spent a whole day in the hospital after gaining consciousness, he was feeling a lot more different than the time he was in his job. He was not missing Kriti anymore but some part of him wanted to take revenge. After a lot of thought, he decided that he had only himself to blame, Abhi had always told him not to take girls too seriously but he did. Then he drank too much at the party that he could not control himself. Then, of course those bullets, which he could call pure bad luck, but by that time, he was feeling quite good to take them to save his friend, actually, best friend.

"Hey, whats up?" Abhi entered in the room when Roshen was thinking of him. *Think of the devil.*

"Nothing, I wanted to talk to you."

"Hmm" said Abhi dragging the chair near Roshen's bed.

"I called my home today. Told them I don't have a job now."

"Oh, how did they take it?"

"Quite well. However what I told them was not true. I said I don't like the job; I would do my own business or may be MBA first then some even better job. They were not happy of course, but they supported me."

"They had no other option."

"Ya, but they were saying that if I don't have a job, I should come back home."

"Don't tell me you want to go home now. I can't live alone."

"I told them that I am still working because there is one month's notice period so I would have to do it without salary. So for one month, I am going nowhere, but if nothing comes up till then, I would have to go."

"Don't worry. I would find you a far better job in one month." Abhi smiled and so did Roshen.

"One more thing, the person who tried to kill you, may try again. So you should be watchful now."

"Yeah, I talked to Mike about that. He said may be my uncle would try to kill me because of property but I still don't think so."

"Dude, please tell me what this property is. You never told me that you are from a royal family. I have been living with a prince for so long and I did not even know that."

Abhi smiled again. He never told his friends about his being from a royal family. But Roshen was something more than a friend now to him. *He almost lost his life for me; he has a right to know.* Abhi took a deep breath and started telling a story he always avoided telling anyone.

"Look, my great grandfather got a lot of property when he was dethroned from being a ruler of a relatively small state, and that property is worth billions now. All that property came to my grandfather and then my father according to my grandfather's will. Actually the property was divided in many pieces but the major one always belonged to my father. Unfortunately, my uncle Ranjit, my father's younger brother, never got any significant part of the property because he never obeyed my grandfather and did not marry according to his wish. But he was living with our family and using all its assets as his own and nobody objected. But uncle always wanted to expand this property, use it for business. My father never allowed him to do that." Roshen was listening carefully. Abhi continued,

"When my father died, he got an opportunity to use this property as he wished. But a huge property without any declared owner came under legal problems. Then every relative and friend of my father tried to claim some amount of this property. One woman even came saying that my father had married her before he died. But she took her claim back; probably she understood that she wouldn't get anything without significant proof. Now the case has been going on for about a year and last week the property was sealed by court until the case is resolved."

"That means if you get this property, you would become a billionaire." Roshen tried to count number of zeros in a billion. *All my life I was trying to get a job several thousand per month and this guy is getting a billion without doing anything.*

"Yes"

"Then I am sure your uncle tried to kill you. He will be the clear owner if you die and anybody can kill anyone for such huge amount of money."

"I don't think so. How can anyone kill somebody for money? "

"How can you say that? You know people are being killed for money daily. People are ready to kill for few hundred rupees."

"Yes, because they don't have any money. Ranjit uncle has a lot of money and when I am not there, he is the owner."

"Exactly Abhi, when you are not there."

Abhi was silent for a moment. First time he did not have any argument against Roshen. Perhaps during all the time they were not together, Roshen was using his mind a lot. Or may be some brain switch inside him was suddenly 'on' by all these happenings.

"Abhi, about what age is your uncle?"

"About fifty five."

"Clearly not a man who uses internet or computer a lot."

"I think so, what do you want to say?"

"Look, the person who came to kill you, has not seen you in person or your photo."

"Yes, that's why he shot you instead of me."

"That means the person who sent him did not have your photo, and if he uses internet, there are many pictures of you scattered on internet on orkut and facebook and on your blog."

"But he is my uncle, how could he not have any picture of mine?"

"Think about it, you left home when you were very young. Then as you said you hardly used to talk to your father. Then I guess your father did not have many pictures of you."

"Hmm..."

"Then how could your uncle have any, you don't go to parties and social gatherings much. So there is a chance that he did not have any pictures of you."

Abhi once again was silent. Roshen's arguments were making sense to him for the first time.

"I am still not sure."

"I don't think you can't have many enemies who don't have your picture and have the guts to try to kill you. Its quite clear I guess."

"Well if he is trying to do that, I am sure I won't let him take a penny of this property." Abhi was trying to think when he had last met his uncle. He saw him last at his father's funeral. For Abhi, he was just another member living in the house and he never cared what he was doing. But now he was trying to recall every little thing he knew about that man.

"Anyways, I need some help. I need to send money home. Can you send it? I will give you my address. Take out some money from my account. My ATM is in the cupboard in my room. And take some to pay bills of the hospital." Roshen knew Abhi won't take money for that, but he wanted to be honest on his part.

"Well, I am not paying your bills here."

"Then who is paying? Priya!"

"Nah, your company. You were a part of it when you were shot, so they are supposed to pay for you." Abhi winked and Roshen understood Abhi was using his insurance given in the company incentives, *evil genius.*

COMING BACK HOME

In a few days, Roshen was discharged from the hospital. The time he spent in the hospital was a much needed break from his life where he spent a lot of time being with himself and analyzing where his life is actually going. He started to reconsider the way he was living his life, always trying to get a stable life, a job, a home and a wife, which used to be his ultimate target, now when he lost all the progress he made, he was thinking perhaps that was not the way life is meant to be and he had a perfect example in front of his eyes, who was taking him back to his apartment, Abhi.

When Roshen entered the apartment, it was looking a lot different than it used to be. The hall which was always empty except some trash was completely clean now and there were posters and paintings lined up on the walls. There was a dustbin in the corner which was full of trash telling that someone had really worked hard to clean the apartment. *What had happened to Abhi?*

Roshen was amazed how Abhi could make an effort to clean the apartment. He always wanted that but he knew that it would look the same after a few days again, so there was no point cleaning. But soon after his entering the apartment, Priya came out from Abhi's room and Roshen understood that it was not Abhi who had done it. *He is complete idiot, such a wonderful girl loved him and he was rejecting her, God knows what he wanted.*

"Welcome back, I hope you are fine now." Priya said with a smile.

"Yeah, just a little pain. It is just a matter of time now." Roshen said who smelled freshly cooked food in the apartment.

"Come on now, I am starving. It took a lot of time to clean your apartment. How do you people make this much mess?"

"It's an art, you should understand, you are an artist." Abhi said while they moved towards Abhi's room.

Roshen was again surprised when he entered in Abhi's room. This was a room where there used to be no space to put a foot and even move inside one had to be careful. Now it had a new carpet on a clean floor. The books were gone and the bed was, like the way it should be. The table was cleaned and laptop was placed on it and walls were missing posters but one thing was the same, Monalisa was still inverted. Priya tried to put it straight but Abhi did not let her do that.

"Wow, this room has changed a lot."

"Yeah, when I was cleaning the blood stains, I figured that this room needed some change. I cleaned your room as well but there was nothing much to do." Priya said.

"Where are all your books? You hid them somewhere?"

"No, I sold them."

"What! But why?"

"Actually I am having some money problem. The property was sealed and there was not much in my account so I sold them."

"You are crazy, you could have asked me. I still have some in my account."

"We can have lunch first, and then we will talk about it. Hurry up, Mike is also coming to discuss about tomorrow's hearing; I don't want to make one more share of this food. It would hit my stomach hard." Said Abhi and sat down on the floor and started opening the packed food. Clearly he did not want to answer Roshen's that question.

Soon they were busy eating and chatting which made the environment very light. For Roshen, it felt like home once again. After a long time he was having homemade food sitting at a place which was now familiar to him and with friends equal to family. Abhi started telling one the story when the previous day he met the police inspector and he offered him to take some protection since they were still trying to find the person who attacked Roshen but Abhi rejected his offer jokingly saying that he wouldn't like some person all the time behind his ass.

Soon after they finished their food, Mike was there. They were still chatting sitting on the floor and Mike sat on the bed. The cleaned room was serving a good purpose of a conference room otherwise in its condition few days back, it would have been impossible to seat four persons, but now that room was cleaned and arranged, there was a lot of space for everyone.

"Are you prepared for tomorrow? It is a big day for this case. The judge is going to hear your uncle's claim tomorrow." Mike asked Abhi after everybody was seated.

"It is you who should be prepared. I don't have anything to do in there except see you shouting at the judge all the time."

"For God sake Abhi, be serious. A lot is at stake in this case for you; and for me as well."

"I know that." Abhi said licking his fingers though he had finished his food more than fifteen minutes ago.

"Do you realize, there may be a lot of foul play from other side? A person who tried to kill you would try everything he could for this property."

"First of all, we don't know who tried to kill me. But I know there is a good chance that Ranjit uncle tried it but I want to be sure first. There are many other claims to this property as well so anyone can try to kill me."

"I am sure tomorrow you will know everything. The way your dear uncle would try to get this property would give you a clear indication how badly he wants it." Mike was quite sure that there would be few surprises in the courtroom next day.

"Did the police get the person who tried to kill me?" Roshen could not keep quiet for long. The image of the shooter was still fresh in his eyes.

"Not yet, I spoke to inspector Ashwin before coming here. He said they have identified the person and trying to get hold of him as soon as possible."

"But how could they identify him without my help?"

"Well, it turned out that it was not just you who saw him the day he came. His name is Bhupendra Singh. He was in the police records and has been arrested several times already for some small charges. And Abhi, this may well interest you that a few days back; your uncle's lawyer got him out of jail when he was in for beating some shopkeeper."

"Wow, why didn't you tell me that before."

"I was coming to it and I am going to use this fact against your uncle in court also."

"And when will I start getting my money. I already have problems without it."

"It depends on the court, I can file a request but I think that would show how much you depend on this money. I guess that wouldn't be a good idea in this situation. Your uncle might use this fact against us saying that you are not capable of earning without this property."

"But who identified the shooter. I thought no one saw him except me." The question was still disturbing Roshen.

"It was me." Priya said who was silent since Mike came in.

"I saw him when I came to drop Abhi at the apartment. He was leaving when I was sitting in my car; his attire caught my attention as well as the drops of blood on it."

COURT HEARING

Many times in life there is a situation when you don't want to do what you can do and you can't do what you want to do. Roshen was now unemployed and did not want to start a job search again but this was only way out for him to proceed. The next day when Abhi, Mike and Priya were all going to the court for the hearing, they made Roshen take rest at home. However Mike assured him that he would be going there on the next date as they would need him to testify about the murder attempt.

Though Roshen was not happy to sit back in the apartment, it gave him time to start looking for what he had to do again, a job. He took Abhi's laptop and started updating his resume on various job portals. He felt that he had made a complete fool of himself when he let such a good job go from his hands. He knew it was absolutely his fault but still he wanted someone to blame on. *Only if Kriti were not there!*

For two hours Roshen kept working on the laptop, looking for jobs, reading blogs, news but then he got bored. He was feeling hungry as well. He called a restaurant and ordered some food but he was still feeling dejected. For a moment he thought of calling home and telling his parents everything but he knew it would alarm them. After all this, he hardly talked to his parents and that also only when it was necessary.

Roshen went to Abhi's room and took a packet of cigarettes and started smoking. He tried to think of the future but his mind went absolutely blank. Something inside him was trying to stop him from taking a similar job again but he did not know what the alternative option is. Somehow the cigarette was giving him some comfort in that situation. *I can ask Abhi for some money and then start my own business.* But Roshen knew that doing business was not really his cup of tea. He was so bad in managing himself that he managed to screw up everything he had in a span of few days only.

Roshen was still waiting for the delivery of the food which was taking more time than usual. Now he was feeling a lot more hungry. He took Abhi's laptop once again and started applying for several jobs and filling some forms. He read on the internet that an earthquake had hit Haiti which was already among the poorest in the world with more than eighty percent of its public living below poverty. The thought of hungry people being hit by disaster made him feel like he himself was starving. He called the restaurant once again and was told that the food is on its way and will reach him any moment. Roshen felt a little angry with their response as it was already more than half an hour since he had ordered the food but there was little he could do on the phone except scolding the person on the other side who took the scolding as if Roshen was blessing him. *Businessmen! They would smile even if you slap them.*

Roshen started wondering about what was going on in the courtroom. Mike was quite sure that there would be surprises. A person who tried to kill someone would do anything he could to get a big share of the property. Roshen thought that he could testify in the court that the person who tried to kill him told him that he was killing for Abhi's uncle before shooting him. Though he did not have anything personal against that man but the direct attack on his life involved him in the case against Abhi's uncle and now Roshen hated him as much as Abhi did, perhaps more. *Had things differently happened. I could have been dead by now.*

Before Roshen could think of anything else, he heard the doorbell. Since he had been shot, he had realized it would be a good idea not to invite trouble by keeping the doors of the apartment closed. So he had bolted the door from inside when Abhi left in the morning. The doorbell was a welcome break to his thoughts as he was more ravenous now than when he called the restaurant. He stood up slowly trying not to put much strain on the injured part of his stomach, took some money out of his wallet and walked to open the door.

When Roshen opened the door, he was surprised to see that it was not the delivery person with food; instead it was a man aged more than fifty with colored hair but partially white mustache which gave away his age. Roshen knew who he was but never expected him to be there.

He was Roshen's father.

It was not a pleasant time in the court for Abhi. Instead of showing how strong his uncle's claim was, his lawyer was trying to weaken

Abhi's claim. Of course he told the judge that Ranjit Yashwardhan was the most eligible candidate to handle the property after the death of Rakesh Yashwardhan but he spent more time on telling the court how inappropriate it would be if the property went to his only son, Abhimanyu Yashwardhan.

Abhi was sitting on a hot platform all the time. There were a lot of personal remarks by the opposition lawyer him. Every small incident from his life which could show that Abhi was not a responsible person was developed in a big story of Abhi's failure. He presented Abhi as an inconsiderate, careless boy who did not know what he wanted to do and always ended up in destroying someone's life or career. The incident when he stole alcohol from his father's bar with his friend and got beaten by him and how that friend eventually committed suicide after coming out of a rehabilitation centre, the incident in his college when he throw a bottle of beer at the warden and was prohibited from entering the hostels for the session, how he was jobless and was using this property to drink and party all the time and at last he gave the example of how his new roommate, who was a simple guy who had lived with Abhi for several months and had ruined his livelihood by behaving crazily and slapping his boss.

Abhi always wanted to say something whenever any remark was being made about him but Mike always stopped him saying that their chance would come. All the stories told about Abhi were true but they were manipulated to show Abhi as a villain in each of them. Mike knew that Abhi had an explanation for everything but the way the opposition lawyer was telling all the things, it was quite clear that he had done his homework well and doing anything stupid might seriously harm their chances in the case.

After the court was adjourned and the next date was announced which was more than two weeks later, Abhi was fairly angry with Mike as he did not react when Abhi's character was being tarnished in the court room. Mike was also upset with Abhi who had been so mischievous in the past.

"So this is how I am getting this property. One person tells the courtroom full of people in front of judge all the bad things happened in my life and proves that I am a pathetic loser who is not mentally balanced and you don't raise a finger at him." Mike was facing Abhi's anger after they were coming out of the court.

"I never told you that the case would be free of dirt. These things happen very often here and nobody takes them seriously until the judge approves of it."

"So you mean that a person accusing me of being one of the worst people in this world who does not deserve to live in society is a 'normal' thing."

"I am not saying that it is normal. I am saying that it is just the opinion of one person who does not want you to win this case and it does not really matter."

"So you are trying to say that it won't make any difference on this case."

"Of course it will. It is a part of the procedure and we have to prove all these accusations wrong."

"Then why were you silent? Why did not you say anything in the court? Is this how you are going to prove it wrong?"

"How was I supposed to know that you have been so notorious in your past? How could I defend you when I did not have anything to say about those stories? Have you ever told them to me?" Mike's tone was a little angry this time. He was already tired of doing every little thing for Abhi in this case and now Abhi was telling him how to do his business. But soon he realized that Abhi was a person who suffered some serious personal remarks about him for a one solid hour so it was not entirely his fault. Anyone would be losing his mind after this treatment.

"Look, it's not like your image has been proved to be bad in front of the court, we will have our say in the next hearing and by that time, I am sure you will tell me many stories showing you are as good a person as I think."

"If I don't have stories, I will make them in next fifteen days." Abhi said with a determination as he left Mike to join Priya in her car. *She must be waiting.*

Sometimes life teaches you a thing better than any teacher could possibly do; a lesson that we start learning when we start to grow up, pretend to fully understand it in front of everyone but somehow forget it, *family comes first.*

Roshen was surprised and scared at the same moment when he saw his father at the door. *How could he come here without telling me, how does he know my address, does he know everything?* There were lot of questions in his mind but before they could be answered, he knew that he was still a son and his father, deserved some respect. He bowed down, touched his feet and took his suitcase to welcome him in his home, an apartment which was now in a shape to welcome a family member, *courtesy Priya.*

Roshen's father, Mr. Akhilesh, was a self made man who was always proud of the fact that he had led his life based on sound principles and never in his life had he done a thing that might bring disgrace to him or his family. Roshen was his only son who had always worked hard to fulfill his expectations and he always felt that he was lucky to get such a son until he got a letter written by his roommate telling him how he bad he was doing actually in his life.

Just one day earlier, he was wondering why Roshen had decided to leave the job when he got it after so many efforts but he made his mind to support his son in every possible way whatever he did. Then he got a letter from some guy named Abhi who had written that Roshen just got broken up with a girl and shattered, he had behaved badly in his office party and got fired from his job and very next day, met with an unfortunate accident. The letter also said how bad Roshen was always feeling to let his family down and he was feeling even worse because he could not tell his parents these things. Tears started flowing from Roshen's father's eyes before he could finish the letter and he took the next flight to reach the address given in the letter.

Roshen came to his room silently guessing what might have caused him to come here when his father followed him inside. A sight of his son having bandages on his hand was quite disturbing already but he did not say anything. He wanted Roshen to speak while Roshen waited for his father to do the same. Roshen saw his father coming in and sitting on the bed. After a few minutes of awkward silence, Roshen decided to speak first but before he could open his mouth, his father did.

"Why didn't you tell us?"

His father was looking into his eyes. It was an emotional moment. Roshen loved his father more than anyone in the world. He was both a strict guardian and a great friend and Roshen was feeling guilty about now not having told him anything. *He supported me when I told him that I was leaving this job, he would have supported me if I had told him the whole truth.*

Roshen never thought that looking into his father's eyes would be difficult some day. He bowed his head as he did not have any answer to the question but in a few seconds, he saw that his old man's eyes were wet.

"I am sorry papa."

Roshen managed to speak those words with a crumpled face and sat on the bed besides his father. His father tried to smile and moved his hand across Roshen's hair and then gently squeezed his cheeks as if he wanted to say, *Look, my son is grown up.* He lunged forward and hugged him which hurt Roshen a bit because of his injury but nothing gave him more comfort than the hug from the person he loved most in this world. After a long time, he was feeling relaxed.

PROPOSAL

Roshen's father did not stay for long. After talking to his son for few hours, he decided to leave as a closed shop for one more day would harm his business a lot. He asked Roshen to come with him but Roshen said that he still had things to do there and would come back as soon as possible. *I can't leave till case is decided.* Roshen's father did not insist on his coming back too soon; he knew that Roshen was now capable of taking his own decisions. Though he wanted to meet Abhi once, he was thankful to Abhi who, through his letter or perhaps with the help of his writing skills, made it possible for them to communicate. Roshen got a word of caution from his father but this time his father was feeling more assured about his son that he would do something good in his life.

Roshen came back after seeing his father off at the airport. He was now feeling more relaxed than before and was thankful to Abhi. For a moment he thought that this move by Abhi could have gone against him. Papa could have reacted differently. But he knew that as his parents, they had the right to know what was going on. When he came back to the apartment, his friend was sitting with a girl he thought was perfect for him but Abhi did not realize it that time. Mike was also sitting there but he was busy making some notes.

"You asshole, you wrote letter to my father and did not tell me." Roshen shouted before entering the room. Abhi was busy in some discussion with Priya at that time and Roshen was almost sitting on him.

"Dude, control yourself. Did someone give you money to kill me?"

"I will kill you without money, you idiot. You are too damn good. You know my father came today."

"Great, where is he?"

"He left. But what made you write a letter about me to him?"

"I just thought it would be nice if someone in your family knows what you have been doing all this time. It's very difficult without family, I know that."

"Hmm, how were things in the court?" Roshen asked sitting besides Abhi.

"Worse than we thought. His uncle made a very strong case to support his claim." Priya said who was not intrigued by their friendly play which interrupted their discussion.

"And I made a fool of myself in the court in front of everyone." Abhi remembered the scene when everyone in the courtroom turned to look at him when the lawyer was telling stories about his life.

"Why, what happened?" Roshen asked.

"Every story in Abhi's life which can in any way indicate that Abhi is not responsible enough to handle this property was told there."

Priya's tone said that she was also very angry with the statements made in courtroom.

"Do you think that I made your life bad in any way? Am I spoiling you?" Abhi was pointing to Roshen.

"Who says that? You are my best friend and you never did anything wrong."

"Well, my dear uncle's lawyer says that I spoiled not only your life but the life of everyone who made a mistake of coming close enough to me."

"That's ridiculous. You are a great guy and I can testify that in the court. You just brought me a lot closer to my family. No friend has ever done this big a favor to me."

"Well, I think now you have another good reason to believe that it was your uncle who tried to kill you." Priya spoke who knew that at the moment Abhi hated his uncle a lot more than he earlier did and would now accept anything against him.

"Yeah, if he wanted the property this badly he could accuse me of being such a bad fellow in front of everyone; I guess he was the one who tried to kill me."

"If you want I can lie in the court that the killer told me he was sent by Abhi's uncle." Roshen was curious to know if this could work.

"Are you crazy?" Abhi spoke, "I don't want you to make false statements and get in some trouble"

"And that would also initiate a long procedure of an attempt murder case against his uncle and it will push you further in problems." Mike said who was finished with his paper work and was now listening to them.

"So what are we going to do now?"

"That's what we were discussing." Priya said, "Mike said that he would tell great stories about Abhi to prove that he is responsible enough to take care of this property. But Abhi is still not convinced."

"Yes, I am not convinced because most of the things he said were true in some sense. I never stayed in a job long enough. I was always living off this property and I have no responsibility towards anyone in this world. I want to change that and I don't think it's possible before the next hearing."

Abhi went silent after saying those words while Roshen's mind started racing in a different direction and then with a smile on his face, he said, "I think it's possible."

"How?" Abhi was looking towards Roshen who had a mischievous look on his face.

"Think about it Abhi, you always said that a job is not a problem for you. I think you can easily get it in twenty days."

"I can get it tomorrow but what is your point?"

"If you have a job before the next hearing and you are married, you are in a respectable position to show the court. You won't be any longer independent, free of responsibilities guy who roams on the city streets, but you would be a married, responsible and self supporting person who is ready to take over his father's property. This would also eliminate the option your uncle has, to kill you and get the property because in your absence, your wife would get the property you should be getting. "

"You don't know what you are talking about." Abhi ridiculed him but Mike was interested,

"I think he is right. But just a job won't tell that Abhi is stable. He should be in the job long enough." Mike said.

"That is not a problem. I have been writing stories for about three years and if you want, I can get a work experience certificate from magazine if I accept their offer to become the editor, I would be in the same firm for more than three years. I guess it is long enough but the marriage idea is stupid."

"Come on Abhi, I can see it. You and Priya are perfect for each other. You two are eventually going to marry some day, why not now?"

"I still think it's not a good idea." Abhi said while Priya was looking at their faces. *It's my marriage and nobody is asking my opinion.* Though she wanted to marry Abhi she never imagined that it may happen this way.

"Abhi" Roshen said, "Do you still remember you owe me one wish?"

"No dude, you can't do this." Abhi sensed what Roshen was about to say.

"Marry her Abhi." Roshen looked in Abhi's eyes and spoke, "You will never find a better girl in your life."

There was a silence for a few moments in the room. Abhi knew what Roshen was saying was right and he had never felt the way he was feeling for Priya in the last few days but it was still awkward to get married this way. Abhi had seen a lot of failed marriages in his own family; his mother committed suicide because his father used to go to prostitutes, his uncle never got married and Priya's mother had also been betrayed by her husband. All that history of unsuccessful marriages always scared him whenever he thought of getting married but he knew it was time to make a decision.

"I want to talk to Priya, alone." Abhi said. Mike moved out of the room briskly while Roshen smiled at Priya and stood up slowly.

Abhi stood up and closed the door. For the first time he was feeling awkward with Priya in a room. Priya was sitting on the bad, still silent. Abhi moved towards her and before she could say anything, Abhi was on his knees in front of her,

"Priya, I know this is not the way you wanted it to be, but believe me, love is the only reason I am saying these words;

Ms. Priya, Will you please marry me?"

Priya hesitated for a moment. She never thought in her life that Abhi would some day propose to her this way. She said the word she had dreamt saying many time in her life,

"Yes"

ENGAGEMENT

Sometimes in life, everything which can possibly go wrong, goes wrong. Sometimes crazy things happen without any crazy output. We don't usually get anything extraordinary out of these situations but we always get a good story. The same was the case with Abhi and Priya's marriage, it was a marriage which was eventually meant to happen but the situation made it quite a special one. Though it was taking lot of efforts to make it happen.

Abhi and Priya decided to get married on twentieth of January which was Priya's birthday as well and eight days before the next hearing. They decided that it would be a very small party with not more than ten people and they would do it in Abhi's apartment as Priya's apartment would attract a lot of attention and hence more guests and even more troubling suggestions. But there was one more person who needed to be convinced before they could actually plan anything.

"I won't approve of this marriage." was Aunt Monika's reaction when Priya told her that she was going to marry Abhi next week.

"Can you tell me one good reason for that?" Priya asked her mother. They were only people in their house that time.

"This is not a joke; you are talking about getting married in such a short time. It's a whole life changing decision."

"This is a decision I made a long time back and you knew about that. Are you telling me to reconsider it?"

"No, I don't have any problem with Abhi. I don't think its right to do all this in such a hurry."

"Why, because it is not conventional? Or you are afraid of what 'people' would say."

"You know I care a lot more about you than this society. I just don't feel that it is the right thing to do." Priya's mother was having a problem finding an argument against her. She never imagined her daughter marrying in such hurry. She always wanted it to be a big ceremony. Also Priya getting married next week would mean that she would be living alone suddenly which would be a drastic change in her life.

"Mom, I know this is not the way you want it to be but believe me, this is the right decision. We can have a huge ceremony later if you want but marriage has to happen now."

"Well, if you have already decided then there is nothing I can do."

"Thank you mom. I love you." Priya jumped. She picked up her phone to tell Abhi and Roshen that the marriage was on. *The bigger task is done, let's prepare now.*

Though they decided that they were not going to make a big affair of this marriage, Roshen decided that he would make the day memorable one for his best friend. *The guy is going to live in a family for the first time in his life, he deserves a treat.* He told Abhi that though the marriage was not going to be a crowded one but it still should be done in a traditional way.

"What exactly you want to do with me?"

"I would call a pundit; everything that happens in a marriage would be done including phereas."

"Can't it be done as an American wedding, you can officiate and then I and Priya would say 'I do' and it's over, short and sweet, isn't it."

"No" Roshen said and Abhi obeyed him like a kid who had just been told by his father that he was not getting his candy.

Meanwhile Abhi went to Mr. Pancholi and told him that he was ready to work as editor of his educational magazine but he would start his work only after the next hearing. He also invited him to his wedding as there was no one else from his side except Roshen. He told Mr. Pancholi that there was no ceremony as such but a very small gathering of close friends. Mr. Pancholi also agreed to certify that Abhi had been working for his magazine and said that he is ready to testify in the court if required. *That is up to Mike if he wants you to*, Abhi told him.

Roshen was taking his responsibility to plan this wedding very seriously. Now when he was unemployed, there was nothing better to do for him anyways and after a rest of several days, he was really looking forward to do something. He decided to decorate the apartment and for that, he bought some lights and got the hall of the apartment painted in sky blue. It was still three days before the marriage when he remembered one thing was missing.

"You people haven't exchanged rings yet." A thing that alarmed

Roshen as he thought of it.

"Dude, I don't have money to buy a ring plus what would happen if we don't do that thing?" Abhi was feeling lazy and the thought of getting married was already making him a little nervous.

"You really don't know anything about marriages, do you? Rings are really very important part of it. This is because one vein from the ring finger goes directly to the heart of a person and this defines the relation between two hearts." Roshen was lecturing Abhi like his father. For the last few days, he had really taken over as his substitute father and Abhi was also giving him all the respect.

"Ok, but what about money?"

"Don't worry, I have the ring. Just tell Priya to get one. We will go tomorrow to her home and exchange them." Finally there was some good coming out of the things that happened with Kriti. The ring Roshen bought for her was destined to have a better fate.

Next day at eleven in the morning, when Abhi and Roshen reached Priya's home, a table full of sweets and Priya beautifully dressed in a green suit with her mother were waiting anxiously for them. She was looking gorgeous and her make-up told that she spent a good time getting ready for this event. For a moment, Roshen felt jealous but he knew that a great guy like Abhi deserved to be someone as wonderful as Priya. Aunt Monika was also happy that marriage was not as eventless as she thought it would be.

"So, what is the plan, are we exchanging rings straightaway or there are some formalities."

"What are you made of dude, we are here to tell you how it will happen. You will do as we would say." Roshen said moving towards Aunt Monika to give her company.

"Okay, so how we are going to do it?"

"Wait for some time, let's have a chat first. I want to decide the amount of dowry first, you know what I mean." Roshen winked at Aunt Monika who smiled in turn.

"Hmm, tell me what you want. Whatever I have belongs to Priya."

"What are you talking about? I don't want anything." Abhi, for a moment thought Roshen was serious but then realized that Roshen was kidding.

"Well, first tell me how good your daughter cooks? I want to know whether she is able to take good care of Abhi or not." Roshen was delivering those dialogues as a perfect actor in character of Abhi's father.

"Look at all these sweets. Priya herself made all of them." Aunt Monika said with an accent of an old woman enjoying the role of a mother trying to get her daughter engaged. Abhi smiled, he knew Priya could paint those sweets but can never cook any of them. Roshen meanwhile continued with his drama,

"We want a car and lots of gold. Can you afford it?"

"We are too poor samdhiji; can't you manage with a cycle and some brass?"

Both Abhi and Priya were smiling seeing two of them acting like that. All four were enjoying this melodrama. Roshen tried to look angry at Aunt Monika's words.

"Get up Abhi; we are not going to have this engagement until our demands are fulfilled."

Abhi did not know how to react. *Am I a part of this drama?* But he did not need to; Aunt Monika spoke before he could say anything,

"Okay okay, I will give you a bike and some silver, will that work?"

"No way, I will take only pure gold."

"I don't have it; please have mercy on us poor souls."

"No, we will take fifty kilogram gold, and that's your daughter. Abhi! Get up and put the ring on her finger and make this gold yours for the rest of your life." Roshen ordered Abhi like a commander. Everybody smiled along with Abhi.

"Do it dude, whom are you waiting for?" Roshen said again to Abhi who was still smiling.

"Give me the ring first you idiot." Everybody laughed once again. Roshen chuckled and took the ring out from his pocket and looked at it for a moment. *I bought it for Kriti.* Roshen knew that it was for the good that the ring was still with him. He felt proud giving it to Abhi.

Abhi leaned towards Priya who quietly moved her hand forward. Abhi put the ring on her finger and whispered with a smile,

"I love you."

"I love you too." Said Priya as Aunt Monika gave her a ring which she slid in Abhi's finger. Her eyes were shining as her dream was coming true. *You are formally mine now.*

TENSION

Finally the day of marriage arrived and Abhi's nerves were toying with his emotions. Today he was going to do a thing the concept of which he had hated all the time, that also in a way that he surprised himself this time. Roshen was doing everything required to perform for the ceremony and this gave Abhi more time to think which was not helping as all the theories he had held against marriage all his life were coming back to haunt him and there were plenty of them.

Roshen, on the other hand was enjoying himself in all the preparations. He selected a suit for Abhi, called a pundit to perform the marriage, prepared a CD with the collection of his favorite songs (*minus sad songs of course as it had to be played at the wedding; it was difficult task for Roshen as most of the songs he liked were those which make people cry*) and was now deciding the menu of the dinner at night.

"How many people have you invited Abhi?" Roshen asked Abhi

when he finished making the menu in which he added more than ten items in the main course even when he knew that less than ten people were coming. He did not notice that Abhi was sitting silently for a long time even though they were in the same room for more than an hour.

"Just Mike and Rohit Pancholi, owner of my magazine. I doubt whether even he would come." Abhi said. He was still thinking about things that would follow after this marriage and sex was not one of the things which were prominent in his mind at the moment.

"Okay, so there would only be..." Roshen paused while he was counting in his brain, "...eight people including two guests of Priya. One other will be pundit and I called one boy to prepare the mandap and serve food. He too would eat, so in total we have to order food for ten people, you know what, I think...."

"I think I made a wrong decision." Abhi cut the Roshen's sentence he was barely listening.

"What?"

"I don't think marrying Priya is the right thing to do." Abhi was speaking slowly as he did not have confidence in what he was saying.

"Don't talk rubbish. You don't know what you are saying."

"I know what I am saying. Marriage will make my life even worse. And what if this marriage does not work out. I can't do that to Priya." Abhi was babbling, "This is all stupid. How did I think that I can be a good husband? I am not ready for so much responsibility. I will screw everything up." Words were coming out of Abhi's mouth more quickly than usual when he felt Roshen's hand on his shoulders. He was now standing in front of him.

"So, what do you want? Call off this wedding?" Roshen said in a soft voice.

"Yes. It would be a big mistake going ahead with it."

"So, do you think you can find a better girl than Priya?" Roshen knew how important it was to calm Abhi at the moment and the only way it could be done was by staying calm himself.

"No, but I think Priya can find a lot better guy. I am not suitable for her."

"And will Priya ever be ready to marry someone else?"

Abhi was silent now. He did not have answer to this question. Roshen knew that it was his time to speak.

"Look Abhi, it is very easy to panic. Marriage is the biggest decision of one's life but believe me, I have seen the two of you together. Nothing makes more sense than the fact that you are meant for each other. Priya loves you a lot and so do you. I know you; you will be a great husband and one day a great father as well. No one can make Priya happier but you."

Abhi felt a lot more comfortable listening to Roshen's. The element of doubt regarding this marriage was now disappearing but he was still silent.

"Don't worry, everything will work out. Now if you let me go, I have to decide the dessert and decorate the apartment also. That stupid boy Raju is still not here." Roshen said and took his mobile phone out and went out to make a call. Abhi kept looking at him as he left. Roshen had been acting like a father to him for last few days and this time he did exactly the thing that only a good father could have done.

WEDDING

This was not the first occasion when Roshen was attending a marriage but for the first time he had taken all the responsibility on his shoulders. Though it was a very small ceremony he was giving his best shot to make everything perfect. Their money problem was solved by combining the credit cards of Abhi and Roshen, and there was nothing to worry about funds for about one month.

The marriage was scheduled to start at five in the evening and according to his plan, everything including dinner would end at about ten. Priya came to the apartment with her two friends and her mother. Roshen locked them up in his room and did not allow Abhi to see her until she was ready for the wedding. Abhi was getting ready in his room while Roshen was busy with the decorations taking help of a hired person and in between he was coming to Abhi to help him and tell him how he was looking. He also gave Abhi and Priya clear instructions not to come out of their rooms until five o' clock.

"So, have you seen Priya, How is she looking?" Abhi asked Roshen after changing his third shirt. He was too concerned and did not want to look too bad as he knew Priya would look lot more beautiful than she usually did and he had to be a match to her.

"You will see her soon buddy, just wait for some more time. By the way, change this shirt, it's not looking good." Roshen said and went out to see whether the 'mandap' was ready. Abhi cursed him as he had finally liked a shirt and Roshen had criticized it.

Mike came with the pundit at half past four. As soon as the pundit arrived, he started preparing for the 'havan' to be performed. Everything he asked for was already there and Roshen told the boy with him to help him and do whatever he wanted. *Soon it would be time to start.*

"Wow, you are looking great." Roshen said as he entered Abhi's room. Mike was also standing there. A clean shaved Abhi wearing a complete black suit with black shirt underneath was looking really stunning. Coincidently, his wrist watch was also black.

"I don't think so. Still something is missing." Abhi was not sure this was his best possible attire.

"Did you take a bath today?" Roshen asked.

"Of course, it's my marriage."

"Then don't worry, its perfect." Roshen smiled and put some perfume on Abhi. Abhi also smiled to hide his embarrassment as he saw that Mike was smiling behind him as well.

Soon everything was prepared and Raju came to their room to say that the pundit was calling Abhi. Roshen glanced at the time in his phone, five minutes past five, perfect.

"Lets go Abhi, Its time to get you married." Roshen said as Abhi, who was waiting for the moment for a long time, stood up from his bed.

"I am still nervous." Abhi said as he reached at the door.

"Oh, then shall I cancel everything?" Roshen started kidding again. He was in a great mood all the day.

"Shut up!" Abhi said as he was escorted out of the room by Mike and Roshen with both of them laughing.

As Abhi stepped out of the room in the hall, he was surprised to see how beautifully Roshen had decorated the apartment. Small lights were placed at selected places and some small pieces of mirrors in shape of star, moon and some in circles were hanging on the walls and reflecting the lights in the every corner of the hall. Just in front of the entrance, the mandap was ready and in the right corner, there was a dining table and several chairs. A red carpet was placed from Roshen's room to the mandap and there were red rose petals all over it. Every small space was beautifully used either for decoration or to put something.

A few moments after Abhi sat in the mandap, the door to Roshen's room opened and everybody turned around to see. Roshen put on the music especially chosen for the moment. First Priya's mother came out and behind her, with her two friends Priya walked in a red sari. One of her friends was holding her hand and Priya was walking slowly looking down, taking each step very carefully. Needless to say that all those efforts she made inside Roshen's room to get ready with her friends for more than two hours, made her look more beautiful than Abhi had imagined. He kept staring at her till she sat on his left side in the mandap when he got a light slap on his head from Mike which made Abhi realize that his mouth was open. Roshen was smiling as he changed the music and lowered the volume so that it would not disturb.

All the time when the pundit was busy in getting Abhi and Priya married, Abhi was busy looking at Priya. He had known Priya almost all his life but she never looked this beautiful. When he had to hold Priya's hand in between for some ritual, he felt a different kind of sensation. Perhaps it was because he knew that this time he was holding her hand for a lifetime. He vowed everything pundit told him and that also with a determination not to break any of them in any condition. Then he took 'Pheras' with Priya and after about three hours in which several rituals were carried out and lots of mantras were chanted, they were husband and wife.

After everything was done, they all started to chat while the pundit took his money and left to perform another marriage. Roshen was trying to flirt with one of Priya's friends when the marriage was going on but, he came to know that she already had a boyfriend; *as usual, bad luck!* Mr. Pancholi also joined them about an hour later when things started and was there till the end. He came with a gift and gave it to Abhi before dinner. Mike had a camera and was capturing the special moments in it which reminded Roshen that he forgot a very important thing but as a lawyer, Mike knew that he would need the proof of this marriage to show in the court.

Dinner came just in time when they needed it. Abhi was thankful to Roshen as he had planned everything almost perfect. Without him, this marriage would have been a boring and haphazard one but Roshen had taken care of everything exceptionally well. Abhi and Priya sat at the dining table to have their dinner with Aunt Monika and Priya's friends while Roshen waited with Mike and Mr. Pancholi as there was not enough room for everyone to have food together. Roshen noticed that the smile never left Abhi's face that evening and that made him proud of his decision. *Abhi has done so much for me, I hope I have returned well enough.*

Long after dinner was over, everybody started to leave. Mr. Pancholi and Mike were the first to leave and after that, Aunt Monika left with Priya's friends. It was funny that in this 'vidai', instead of bride, her family and friends were leaving. At twelve o' clock, there were only Abhi, Priya and Roshen in the apartment.

"I think we should sleep now. I am very tired." Abhi said to Roshen, he wanted some time alone with Priya now which was now his right as her husband.

"Sleep! This is your first night together and you want to sleep. What are you, twelve? Have I married two kids?" Roshen was still full of energy even after a lot of work all day long. Abhi saw Priya smiling Roshen's dialogue.

"Dude, sleeping is a metaphor. Now will you please leave the two of us alone? Its midnight and I am a respectable married person. It's not cool to hang out with dudes at this time." Abhi winked to Roshen and then looked towards Priya, "Is it?"

"Not at all." Priya said with a smile.

"Then go ahead, your room is waiting for you." Roshen smiled and pointed towards Abhi's room. Abhi along with Priya did not wait for a moment and went to the room and to their surprise, there was a double bed instead of Abhi's single bed and that was also decorated with flowers. Abhi looked out where Roshen was ready with an explanation.

"I figured out you would need some more space tonight so I shifted my bed in your room and joined it with your bed."

"So where would you sleep?" Abhi asked.

"Sleeping on the floor one night won't hurt me that bad. I have recovered from the injury." Roshen smiled as Abhi shut the door from inside but before he did that, he saw Roshen showing him his thumb as good luck for their first night; *A great friend, indeed.*

DAY AFTER WEDDING

The beauty of life is that it never gives you enough to satisfy. Once you get through with one challenge, there is another waiting for you. Once you cross one door, you get many others to open. Marrying Priya got Abhi only halfway to where he wanted to go. There was a bigger thing to do before he woke up next morning, or rather afternoon as it was after twelve noon when he woke up, his friend Roshen and lawyer Mike had already started working the next step.

When Abhi came out of his room the next day, he saw Mike sitting on the floor with Roshen in the latter's room and they were discussing how Roshen was going to testify in court and the possible questions that he might face there. They seemed quite busy in their conversation with Mike making a note of every point. *So they started working without wasting any time,* Abhi thought.

Abhi went straight to the bathroom when he saw Mike sitting with Roshen. He had a wonderful time the previous night and did not want to ruin his mood by talking about the case, but somewhere inside he knew he had to; so he was trying to delay this conversation as much as possible and going to bathroom was a legitimate way to do that when he just came out of his room after a long night.

"So this way you would well indicate to the court that along with being a helpful guy, Abhi is also the most deserving candidate for the property and somehow somebody else knew it and that's why someone is trying to kill him." Mike was saying while his eyes were on the pad in his hands.

"But what if that lawyer asks me whether I suspect anyone for this murder attempt?"

"Be very careful not to mention any name. You have to show that you are just Abhi's roommate, not a very close friend and you have no idea about this property." Mike was stressing every word like a teacher trying to make his students mug up a definition.

"But I don't think there is any way Abhi is getting the whole property. I mean, his uncle also deserves some part of it."

"It's very difficult but not impossible. Justice Choudhary is famous for his controversial decisions. If we somehow convince him that Ranjit Yashwardhan is a crooked man who can misuse this property, he may end up in getting very small portions."

"What if we can prove that he was the one who tried to kill Abhi?"

"That will make things complicated but in our favor. But it is very difficult until we find some solid proof." Mike said as he turned to see Abhi who entered the room. Abhi's face was glowing with a different kind of spark today and Roshen's mood changed as he saw him.

"How was your night uncle Abhi?" Roshen started teasing him.

"His face is saying everything. Don't you think it is more pink than usual?" Mike joined Roshen.

"Shut up you two. And give me some space to sit." Said Abhi while pushing Roshen on one side.

"Ya, sure. You must be very tired." Roshen said and winked at Mike while Abhi blushed.

"Where is Priya?" Roshen asked on a serious note.

"Still taking rest. So you were talking about the case." Abhi said looking at Mike this time.

"Yeah, Mike has prepared the case for you. He also came up with many good stories about you to tell in the court." Roshen said.

"Yeah, and I want some more if you can tell me." Mike said while Abhi looked at him silently as he was thinking of something.

"There are lots of them. Like he donates money for orphanage, spends time with kids there. In spite of having a palace, he lives in a small apartment." Roshen said with excitement.

"I know all these things. I have enough to speak about him. I just wanted to know if there is something exceptional worth narrating." Mike said looking towards Abhi again.

"What about uncle? Are you telling any of his stories?" Abhi asked instead of answering Mike.

"Of course, at least five big incidents from his life. I want to give him the same dose he gave you that day." Mike said with a lot of pride.

"Don't tell any of those. I don't want any foul play for this property." Abhi said.

"What?" Mike was more than surprised. It was obvious after Abhi's reaction when he had been insulted in the court, anybody would have loved to insult his uncle. And the fact that Abhi was telling him not to do that, after he had done all his research work on Ranjit Yashwardhan was even more annoying.

"Yes, first of all I don't want the reputation of our family to be tarnished this way and secondly I don't think it would serve any purpose telling stories about him. I am sure his lawyer would be prepared with a proper explanation for all of them." Abhi said.

Roshen looked impressed with Abhi's thinking. With only a little involvement, he was producing a good logic about everything. However Mike still did not like that all his efforts were going to be futile.

"As you wish. But I still think it would be a bad idea not to attack him just because you think he would be prepared for it." Mike said.

"Believe me; I know what I am saying." Abhi said. He was thinking about this case more than he showed.

"Ok, I have to go now. And I want to meet Rohit once again. Though I told him that he would need to testify in the court, his part is quite simple, I want to discuss with him as well." Mike said while standing up. He was still thinking about the time he had wasted on gathering information about Ranjit by talking to his old friends, finding every person who hated him and making fake calls to Ranjit himself.

"I am sure he will help you. All the best." Abhi said when Mike was leaving.

"Best of luck to you. It's you who are going to lose if anything goes wrong." Mike said in anger. It was the frustration as the hard work of the previous week was not producing any result. Annoyed, Mike slammed the door before leaving but only to see Abhi smiling inside before the door closed.

THE NEWS

The next few days turned out to be very busy in everybody's life. Abhi was blooming in his newlywed life which felt better than he ever thought. For Priya, she was watching her dream coming true and it was as beautiful as she had expected. Mike was preparing for the hearing, with a little help from Abhi and Roshen. Abhi had already made his task difficult but still he was determined to win this case for him as he was yet to establish himself and this case was a golden opportunity for him. Roshen was busy looking for a new job along with thinking about the case. He had gone for an interview as well but after facing so many interviews, he had a very clear idea about his chances.

"So how does it feel to be married?" Roshen asked Abhi one day before the hearing. They were hardly finding any time alone together after Priya moved into the apartment but Roshen did not mind Priya giving them company. But still it was different when Priya was around as the topics they discussed for the time being, restricted to just the case and property matters. Their apartment also changed a lot within a few days, it was a lot more clean with a girl living there, the hall was full of gifts that Abhi's mother-in-law gave that included a sofa set, a television and a refrigerator a lot bigger than what Abhi had.

That day, when Priya went to see her mom, Roshen and Abhi once again got a chance to talk personal stuff which they never could in front of Priya. Perhaps Abhi was feeling the same way. That's why he was having a beer with Roshen in the middle of the day but this time, Roshen was smoking and Abhi wasn't.

"It's feeling nice right now but I am not sure what will follow." Abhi said in a philosophical tone, "What about you, you seem quite busy these days. What are you doing?"

"Job hunting. I appeared for an interview yesterday but I don't think I will get a chance there."

"Oh, but when did you go? I thought you were in the apartment all the time."

"In the morning, you are always locked up in your room. I did not want to disturb you so I didn't tell you."

"Hmm, if you want I can help you to find a job. I may not be having the property but I still have a few contacts; one phone call from me can do things."

"I know that but I don't want any favors. I want to get a job myself. This job is going to be probably the biggest achievement of my life and I would love it if I can do it alone." Roshen said with a smile on his face.

Abhi was impressed with Roshen's approach. He realized that Roshen had changed a lot since the day he first came to the apartment and a major part of this change occurred after the time he spent in the hospital. That accident definitely changed things for both of them.

"As you wish buddy, just remember I am always with you." Abhi said.

"Anyways, did Mike tell you he met Inspector Ashwin yesterday? That guy who shot me is still absconding and the police have no clue where he is."

"I don't think the police can get hold of him. It's been a month. He must be living in some other city or may be gone to some other country by now and if he is not fool enough, there is no chance that he can be caught now."

"What if he is asked to kill you again? He has to show up then." Roshen was trying to think a way that the man could be caught.

"Yes, maybe we can force him to show up this way, but may be this time he is successful, that would mean endangering my life. I am not sure I want to do that after I have got married." Abhi said. Though he had downed one beer he was still sober.

"Ashwin also interrogated your uncle. He called me yesterday to ask whether I am fine now. He seems to be a nice guy."

"May be he is, but I don't trust many policemen. Most of them would usually do anything if you can give them the amount they want." Abhi said but Roshen thought that he was being judgmental about what he did not know much. They had finished their beers and neither of them was feeling a thing. That prompted Abhi to open two more bottles though he did not know Roshen whether wanted to drink or not but he did not ask, he just felt that Roshen wanted it.

"You know Abhi, you are the only person I drank this much alcohol with. It's strange but I feel that without you, I am a different person." Roshen said changing the topic.

"Now please don't tell me you are attracted towards me." Abhi said, he found Roshen's words silly who, on the other hand was being sentimental.

"What can I do, you are so hot that I can't resist myself in front of you." Roshen said as he knew how stupid his words sound and lunged towards Abhi to scare him. The beer was now showing its effect a little.

"Stop it dude, I am married now." Abhi said showing the ring on his hand and with a smile on his face. Roshen also started laughing and in between the laughter, Abhi heard his phone ringing. *It must be Priya,* he thought.

But it wasn't Priya, it was Mike. Abhi knew that Mike was working very hard for the case and he must be willing to talk something related but he was having such a good time with Roshen that he was not willing to take the call. He pushed the 'silent' button on his phone and threw the phone on the bed and started talking to Roshen again.

"So now I have two options at a..." Abhi was saying when his phone rang again. Abhi looked at the phone, it was Mike again. *It might be something important,* Abhi thought.

"Hello" Abhi said receiving the call.

"Why did you pick up the phone so late?" Mike said on the other end. His voice was louder than usual which alarmed Abhi for a moment.

"What happened?" Abhi's tone changed suddenly which attracted Roshen's interest as well. He also started trying to hear what Mike was saying but his words were hardly audible to him.

"I have a piece of news." Mike's voice was trembling even when he was not drunk.

"What is that?"

"The man, who shot Roshen, Bhupendra Singh, has been arrested."

RANJIT GETS NEWS

"Hello." Ranjit Yashwardhan was answering an unexpected phone call from his lawyer, Tapan, who had been sitting with him just few minutes back discussing about the property. Even though the last hearing went the way he wanted it to, he was not yet satisfied with the progress. Ranjit always wanted the whole property and with Abhi alive, there was a very small chance that he would get what he wanted.

"I have a piece of bad news." The voice in the phone said. Ranjit was hearing a lot of bad news for a long time. His plan to grab the property after the death of his brother was perfect. With Abhimanyu not having any interest in his father's property, all responsibility was supposed to fall automatically on him and nobody would have even noticed that this property did not have an owner. He was the unofficial owner who would become official at some point of time. He was supposed to take over everything slowly giving Abhi whatever he wanted, *just some money every month.* But the claim from a prostitute ruined everything.

"What happened now?" Ranjit was ready to hear the news and then prepare for remedial actions, *a thing he had been doing for last few months.*

"The police have caught Bhupendra."

As words were uttered the phone Ranjit's world was shattered. He never expected that after his clear instruction to stay underground, the police would find Bhupendra. That was a moment of uncertainty. But before taking any decision, there were questions to be answered.

"How did it happen?"

"No idea, but the news is correct. And if he tells the police that you sent him to kill Abhimanyu, you are in big trouble."

"What do you mean by 'you'; it was your idea to kill him. If someone will be in a problem then it's both of us, not just me." There was anger in Ranjit's voice. He was annoyed by the number of problems coming between him and the property.

"Look; I am nowhere in this matter. Killing Abhi was just a suggestion. 'You' are the one who would have benefited from that. Plus you gave Bhupendra an order to kill him; he works for you, not Me." came a sharp reply and the phone was disconnected.

Ranjit Yashwardhan was taken aback by this response. Though he was not yet the owner of the royal property but he still belonged to the royal family and nobody had ever talked to him like that. He was already shocked by the news of the arrest and now his lawyer was no longer with him, perhaps. *Now what?*

Ranjit's mind was racing, thinking of the possible solutions to this problem. Though he was sure that Bhupendra would not tell the police about him easily but there was an element of doubt. *Anybody can be broken,* he always believed.

Getting arrested for the murder attempt was the last thing he wanted. Suddenly the property became his second priority. He wanted to save himself from yet another trial and this time, if it happened, with Bhupendra speaking against him, it would be really difficult to get away. All his dreams were trashed and he was now dreading the worst.

When a situation, a man is not ready to face or does not want to face, comes to him, there is always a universal solution; run. Ranjit, not knowing what to do when the police might come to arrest him any time for attempting a murder for the property, did the same thing. He called his servant Hari after gathering the things required to leave the palace,

"I am leaving, will come back in few days. If anybody comes to visit, tell him I am out of station." Ranjit said and left.

Hari was watching him leave. He sensed that something bad has happened but he did not dare to ask what.

POLICE STATION

Abhi was fighting a battle against his own uncle in which he did not indulge himself by choice. He wasn't even aware of the seriousness of the situation until Roshen was accidently shot when someone was trying to kill him. But the good thing was, in this battle, he was never alone. He had a friend who, though unknowingly, faced the bullets meant for him. He had a love who, without questioning, was a part of every quest he undertook. He had a lawyer who was assiduously trying to win this case for Abhi and he had good luck. Just before the day of hearing, he had found the person who could be key to his win.

Bhupendra Singh had been working for the royal family for a long time, especially for Ranjit Yashwardhan. After he was given the task of killing a person belonging to the family itself, he was a little hesitant. The thought of killing a person whose family was being served by his family for more than a hundred years was a little scary but all these years he had been working with Ranjit Yashwardhan, he always got his rewards and when his master wanted him to do a work of utmost importance, it was not even remotely possible that he could say 'no'. *A person who does not follow his father and lives outside the palace to work for some small company should not belong to a royal family.*

Bhupendra reached the address he was told he would find Abhimanyu Yashwardhan alone. When he saw a person smoking alone in the apartment, he was quite sure that he was the person to be killed but his master did not have his photograph so to make sure, he asked him whether he was Abhimanyu. The answer was a question about his own identity which Bhupendra took as an affirmative answer and did the thing he was supposed to do. *Royal blood must clean royal mud.*

But soon he knew that things had gone horribly wrong. He had shot the wrong person who had survived. *I shot three bullets, how could anyone survive?* But the question at the moment was different. Of course he did not want to face his master's wrath and for that, Bhupendra thought of trying to kill Abhimanyu one more time but his master told him not to. He was told to hide at some place till he got the next order.

For about a month, Bhupendra did the task successfully but it was continuously difficult for him to live underground. He had a family to take care of and without him, his wife and two kids were facing problems. Though money was being provided to his family by his master and there was enough in store so that they wouldn't need any for about a year but he was missing his family a lot and it had been about a month. So there was a very slight chance that police would be hovering around his house. That's where he made a big mistake.

"Did he tell who sent him?" Were Abhi's first words when he

reached the police station with Roshen. Mike was already there waiting for them and it was clear looking at their faces and clothes that Abhi and Roshen had come rushing as soon as they got the news. Their mouths still smelled of liquor and Mike felt a little embarrassed standing with them in the police station but he decided to ignore it.

"I don't know. Even I just came here. I am waiting for inspector Ashwin who told me that he arrested his man. Perhaps he is inside the cell."

"Wow, which means if he says that Abhi's uncle sent him to kill Abhi, Abhi will definitely win the case." Roshen was excited by the news as much as Abhi or perhaps even more because he was the person who had faced the bullets fired by that person.

"I am afraid not. May be Abhi's uncle is the worst person in the world but he still has some right to this property as ..." Mike stopped when he saw someone coming towards them. The person joined them and offered a hand to Mike with whom he had just talked on the phone. He was inspector Ashwin. After Mike he offered his hand to Abhi and Roshen also and before they were done with the handshakes, Mike fired a question to him.

"Did he say anything?"

"Not yet, but don't worry. He has just been caught; his blood is still hot. Soon he will understand how it feels inside a police inquiry room."

"Great job anyway, where did you find him?" Abhi asked. He was least hopeful that the police would have any success finding their guy.

"I appointed one person to see whether he comes back is home and tapped the phone there. Though he came in disguise he called before coming and when he came, we were all waiting to welcome him." Ashwin told Abhi the shorter version of his story which changed Abhi's perception about policemen up to an extent.

"Can we see him?" Roshen asked. He was anxious to see the person who shot him behind the bars.

"I wanted you to see him. This will confirm that we have the right guy. He should also know that the person he almost killed, is not going to spare him." Said Inspector Ashwin and started walking to a gallery outside which eventually led to the cell where a few prisoners were kept. After crossing a few cells, the inspector stopped in front of one where Roshen saw the person for the second time, this time sitting with his head down in one corner. He wore clothes similar to what he had worn the day he shot Roshen. Abhi and Mike were also trying to look at his face closely behind the bars.

"Have a look at the bastard. Now he will spend the rest of his life inside." The inspector said loudly to provoke him. Bhupendra had a look at his visitors, stared them for a few moments and then bowed his head again. He was not interested in those people at the moment. He was just feeling bad to let his master down.

Roshen felt scared by the look of those eyes for a moment but soon he realized that he was the person with a greater control over the situation that time. For the first time, he wanted to kill someone in his life. *One who can try to murder someone for some money, does not deserve to live in society.*

"Inspector," Mike spoke, "tomorrow is the hearing for the property case for which this murder was attempted. If you can make him speak today, it would be great for us."

"I realize how important it is for you that this person tells us who sent him. I bet he will tell us everything today." Inspector Ashwin said with a smile. He did not notice that the person inside was also smiling as he heard his words. *You lost my dear; I will never speak against my master.*

FIRST FIGHT

The next few hours were very long for everyone related to the royal property. The news of Bhupendra being arrested alarmed Ranjit Yashwardhan and he was thinking of the consequences sitting all by himself. Abhi and Roshen started to analyze the situation to help Mike to figure out how to make the best of this progress. Inspector Ashwin was trying to make a person speak who made himself dumb for the time being and Bhupendra was at the receiving end of every mental and physical effort made by the police to make him speak.

It was three in the afternoon when Abhi and Roshen came back to their apartment. Mike wanted to prepare for the hearing so he wanted some time alone. He told Abhi that he would come and meet him in the evening. That left Abhi with Roshen to discuss things about the case. Abhi almost forgot Priya, who was back at the apartment by then and was waiting for Abhi when he entered his room with Roshen.

"Where have you been? I have been waiting for you guys for more than half an hour." Priya said as he saw Abhi. She was doing something on Abhi's laptop sitting on the bed. As Abhi saw her, he realized that in all the haste, he had forgotten to tell Priya about the arrest.

"Priya, I have something to tell you." Abhi was full of excitement as he moved towards her. He knew that this news will give her as much relaxation as it gave Abhi and Roshen.

"I know that." Priya quipped.

"How did you know?" Abhi was surprised. *There was no one to tell Priya, how in the world could she know, does she command a network of highly trained spies?*

"Four empty and two half filled bottles of beer. I know you guys were drinking here. And you have taken lunch without me. You went out to eat, am I right?" Priya said at which Abhi almost smiled, Priya continued when Abhi was looking at her,

"Look, I have taken food; If you want to eat some more, it's there in the box. It is okay here, but I will never allow you to make such a mess when we would be living in our house." Priya said in a tone of disappointment as she made food with her mom for Abhi but what he said in the end, surprised Abhi.

The smile vanished from Abhi's face when Priya talked about living at some other than this apartment. Abhi never saw this coming but there it was, just a week after the marriage and things started changing. *That's why I always hated marriage.*

"Well, now I have two things to tell you." Abhi said in a loud voice which he never did while talking with Priya. Roshen was standing silent behind Abhi. Priya's words hurt him a little also but he always knew, sooner or later, it had to happen.

"What happened?" Priya said. She sensed that she had said

something Abhi didn't like. She was now wondering what it was.

"First, we haven't taken our lunch. The police arrested the man who had shot Roshen and we went to see him at the police station." Abhi paused for a moment, Priya wanted to say 'wow' but she realized Abhi wasn't finished yet.

"And the second thing is," Abhi said, "We are never leaving this apartment." This time Abhi was a lot louder which almost made Priya cry; she never wanted to hurt Abhi; neither was she looking forward to leave the apartment. But she knew that somewhere down the road, when they planned to have a family, they would need to leave this apartment. She did not respond to Abhi and there was a silence in the room which was awkward for each of them.

"Wow, this food smells great." Roshen finally broke the silence to change the subject. He also felt that it was a little harsh of Abhi to shout at Priya. He felt that though Priya had married the guy she wanted to, she still wasn't getting what she should have got as a newlywed. *Instead of a honeymoon, she was stuck with this case of property but yet, she never complained.*

Abhi looked at Roshen and suddenly felt that what he did was wrong. Priya must have felt insulted when Abhi said something in front of a friend even though it was Roshen. But he did not want to leave the apartment at any cost. In those moments of uncertainty, Abhi could not think of what to do so he left the room leaving Roshen with Priya.

"I am sorry; I didn't mean to hurt you guys." Priya said with her eyes filled with tears. Roshen felt like moving ahead and wipe those tears off Priya's face but he knew it would make Priya cry even more. None of them was wrong at that time but somehow, everyone was upset.

"It's ok; Abhi is stressed because of this case. Don't take him seriously." Roshen did not want to stretch the topic at the moment. "By the way, we are very close to winning, with the arrest of this guy; I think Abhi's uncle will now spend his time behind bars thinking about the property." Roshen said.

Priya responded with a smile. Roshen also smiled and left the room. He now wanted to talk to Abhi who was sitting on the sofa in the hall, lost in his thoughts.

"Are you upset?" Roshen said sitting besides Abhi. Abhi did not say anything, a sign that showed that he was really upset, very upset.

"Look, what Priya said, wasn't that wrong." Roshen said. Abhi was still silent, after a long wait, he spoke,

"I know Priya is not wrong. I am upset because I knew it would happen. I was right about myself; I cannot become a good husband."

"Who said you are not a good husband. After what happened inside, I think you are a great husband." Roshen said.

"Stop kidding, which good husband shouts at his wife in front of his friend?"

"Many, but only few of them understand how much it hurts when they do so. And you are one of them. What you did in the room was the spontaneous reaction of any person but you soon realized it was wrong, that's why you are a better husband than many others." Roshen said. He had, by now, mastered the art of cheering Abhi up.

"But I don't want to leave this apartment and she does. Don't you think it's a tough situation?"

"Not at all; she doesn't want you to leave the apartment now. You also know that you cannot always live here. Someday, you will have to leave and I have to leave as well."

"Hmm, I know that. I don't want to raise my kids here. This place is not really appropriate for a family." Abhi was convinced now. It was strange looking back, when Roshen had first met Abhi, it had been almost impossible for him to make Abhi listen to him on any issue but now he had taken over the role Abhi used to play in the initial days of their friendship.

"Yeah, and if you win the case, you would be living in a place far better than this one. You don't want any unemployed friend who drinks and smokes in a family, do you?" Roshen said punching Abhi on his shoulder.

"If that unemployed smoker is you, I sure do." Abhi said with a smile which was silently saying 'Thank you' to Roshen.

"Now, are you going to talk to your wife or not? Don't tell me that I have to do it for you." Roshen said for the first time referring to Priya as 'Your wife' to Abhi which made Abhi feel that he was a married person now who just had his first fight with his wife. Just the thought made him smile.

IDEA

In his short career, Inspector Ashwin never came across such a stubborn character. He was a man who had joined the police with sole motive to bring change in society and improve the image of the police force which was always condemned by the public since he saw his father, a constable, dying in a police encounter with some terrorist. Along with his job, he was also preparing for the state administrative services in which he had failed the last few times, but somehow, he had kept himself going, always preparing for a bigger task. His life was now hanging between studies, criminals and family; and by now, he had started feeling that this was too much to handle. That resulted in a kind of frustration which was now being multiplied by the attitude of a person behind the bars.

In the last few hours, Ashwin had tried everything he could on this man but he had sealed his mouth. He refused to talk nonsense. Ashwin tried physical torture but the man was handling it easily. He had tried to make him speak by playing 'good cop-bad cop' but it didn't work. After a few hours of trying, he felt like giving up when his phone rang, it was Mike who was now calling for the fourth time in the last two hours.

"No, he didn't say anything yet." Inspector Ashwin said straightaway as he picked up the phone. He knew why Mike was calling and his answer was disappointing.

"Come on, what are you doing damn it." Mike said on the other end which irritated the inspector even more.

"Well, if you think you can do it better, you are most welcome here." Anger was prominent in his voice which made Mike realize that inspector who had been more than helpful to him this case and there was no doubt he was trying his best.

"I didn't mean that. I am just worried. You know how important it is for him to speak for this case."

"I know that. But please don't call me again. I will inform you as soon as he says anything." Said inspector Ashwin and disconnected the phone before Mike could say anything. He knew he had to go and try even harder. *Everyone has a threshold; I just need to cross his.*

Being a couple is not very simple but when you love someone, marriage becomes the easiest and most helpful relationship to base a life on. And with a friend like Roshen, Abhi had a great support alongside to make this marriage work whenever little dispute arose, but the at the moment there was another piece of news which Mike told them and that upset all three of them, Bhupendra had refused to talk.

"So how exactly we are going to tackle this case if he doesn't say anything?" Roshen was curious to know as it was going to be his chance to turn up in the witness box but things were pretty uncertain at the moment and Abhi had no answer. Priya was listening intently as all of them sat in Abhi's room after receiving Mike's call.

"I have no idea, only Mike will be able to tell us." Abhi said. He was trying to think of all the available options.

"Is he coming here?" Roshen asked.

"No, he said he was going to see Inspector Ashwin. He was also quite upset. The inspector was not talking to him properly and he said he would like to see what he was doing at the police station. Maybe his presence would pressurize the inspector to do something."

"I think we should also go there." Priya said.

"What will we do there? We cannot make that bastard speak." Abhi was a bit reluctant to follow Priya's suggestion as he just had a fight with her.

"I think Priya is right. Maybe our being there would show the inspector, how important it is for us that this person talks today and then he would make some extra efforts. If nothing else, we can discuss the case with Mike." Roshen supported Priya.

"Okay then, let's go." Abhi said. He knew it was difficult to argue when both Priya and Roshen were on the same side.

"Any progress?" Abhi said as he saw Mike at the police station. He was sitting alone on a desk near the entrance.

"Not yet, I personally went in and saw him. Seems like there is no way they can make him speak. Perhaps he knows how important it is for everyone." Mike said. He was also tired of waiting and had already made up his mind what he was going to do the next day.

"So are we going to refer to it in court tomorrow?" Roshen asked.

"No, I had prepared everything assuming that he would take Ranjit's name but now I think we cannot use him as evidence. I just hope that before this case is over, we somehow get some proof against Abhi's uncle. Or he will get a lot more share in this property than he deserves." Mike said.

"So that means I will have to testify in the court tomorrow." Roshen was anxious to know what his role was going to be, as a spectator or an actor in the show.

"Yeah, but I still hope if we could make Bhupendra speak, it would be a great advantage. We still have all night." Mike said.

"No, we don't have all night." A voice spoke behind them. Everyone along with Mike turned to see who it was. It was Inspector Ashwin who just came from the cell after a one sided conversation with Bhupendra and now was feeling that he was making a fool of himself by even trying.

"Why are you saying that? Did he say anything?" Mike asked.

"Nah, and I don't think he is going to talk today. Press people wanted to talk about this case and I told them I will speak to them at nine o' clock. It is already eight thirty and there is no way we can do it before nine."

"So you are telling me you won't try after it is nine." Mike said looking in the eyes of the inspector which he certainly didn't like.

"No" came a sharp reply.

"So you are working to show the media. You know it can change everything if he speaks today and even than you are acting like this." Mike said. For a moment, he forgot that this was not his court, but a police station where the inspector could have told him to get out any moment he wanted to.

"Don't tell me how to do my duties. I am burning my ass in this police station for last thirty six hours and if you think there is any way you can make him talk, you are most welcome but don't give me that crap in my police station." Inspector Ashwin lost his temper when he heard Mike talking like that. Everybody was silent before Priya interrupted.

"But we still have some time. Instead of fighting, if we try and think of something to make him talk or maybe we can find some evidence which may prove this person's relationship with Abhi's uncle."

"Even if we can find some link, that wouldn't prove that Ranjit sent this guy to kill Abhi. We need some solid evidence." Mike said only to find that no one was listening to him except Roshen. Abhi sat down in one corner lost in his thoughts. He was unusually silent during the conversation.

"So I guess this is it." Mike spoke again, "Tomorrow I am going to go with the speech I prepared a few days back. Roshen, you are going to tell the court that Abhi is a great guy and I will remind Mr. Pancholi that he also needs to be there in the court room."

There was a disappointment in his tone. A progress which could have won them the case and that also earlier than they imagined was proving to be futile. Roshen turned around to see Abhi who was still sitting on the bench thinking something. Priya's face also missed spark he had always seen there.

"Okay guys, I am sorry. I am trying once more before I talk to the press. I think he will eventually speak. It's just a matter of time." Said Inspector Ashwin as he turned to go in again when he heard Abhi's voice the first time that night.

"I have an idea." Abhi said.

Everyone looked at him. They were excited to know if Abhi had really thought of some possibility which could make Bhupendra speak which was proving to be impossible for the inspector himself. For the next few minutes, Abhi told them what there was in his mind and tried to convince everyone that it could work.

RANJIT'S REACTION

The next morning, when sun rose, it brought bad news for Ranjit Yashwardhan who was sleepless all night, in a house he owned just outside the city, thinking about the arrest of Bhupendra Singh and consequences of it. Though he was doubtful that Bhupendra would say anything against him but he knew that a person who looked strong on the surface, might sometime give up against physical torture. Besides, he knew that physical torture wouldn't be the only thing he would be facing, the police would try certain tricks against him as well and there was no way he could have saved him. Bhupendra's arrest was non-bail able and everyone he approached raised their hands giving one reason or the other. Even his lawyer, Tapan did not call him again so no help was to be expected from there as well. *Nobody sails on a sinking ship.*

There was a naked girl whom Ranjit gifted that house few years back lying on the bed. Since then, he came stayed for a couple of days quite often. The bare back of the girl was visible while the lower portion was covered by a quilt. It was only six in the morning but Ranjit had a difficult time in bed as well. All night, his thoughts were occupied as to what would happen in the future. And when he picked the paper up in the morning, he got a clear idea as to what there was in store for him.

Of the two newspapers he saw in the morning, one was local and other was published from the capital. Both of them had the news of the arrest of the person who tried to kill the member of the royal family. In the local newspaper, this news was on the bottom corner of the front page in which, the statement of inspector Ashwin saying that the person had named an important member of the royal family who had sent him and the investigation was still on whereas in the other paper, the same news was in brief and on one of the inside pages.

Last night, when Ranjit called home, Hari told him that two policemen had come asking for him and told him that Ranjit Yashwardhan had to report in the police station as soon as he came back. There was no doubt in Ranjit's mind that Bhupendra had confessed everything and now the police was looking for him.

This whole history appeared before Ranjit Yashwardhan's eyes, especially the way his brother always kept him away from property. Every demand of Ranjit was being met but he was never allowed to have the power he always wanted in his hands. His brother, the favorite child of his father, got every power and always either misused them or did not use them all.

All ambitions of Ranjit Yashwardhan were being thwarted by his elder brother's amusements. When, one day Rakesh Yashwardhan was confined to bed because of consuming excess of alcohol, Ranjit thought of a possible way in which he could get all the property. He started indulging himself in the small deals related to the property and declared himself the owner while he slowly kept poisoning his brother which eventually led to his death.

Nothing went according to plan after the death of his brother. After finding out that Rakesh Yashwardhan had died without a will and some woman had claimed his property saying that she was his widow every friend of Rakesh, every cousin and uncle and each person related to him anyhow claimed his property and in this process, Ranjit's nephew and Rakesh's son, Abhimanyu, also did the same which alarmed Ranjit because he never thought it would happen given the kind of life Abhi was leading by now and everything Ranjit knew about him.

The plan to kill Abhimanyu and then get the entire property went wrong and now Ranjit was on the verge of being thrown out of the property and getting arrested as well. *I always deserved better, he thought. Life never did justice to my talent.*

Thinking all this, Ranjit sat down on the other side of the bed where the girl with whom he spent his last night and lot of others, was still sleeping. Ranjit looked at her but her bare body hardly distracted him. He slid his hand under the pillow where he had hidden a thing which had been in his possession for last ten years but he never really used it, *his gun.*

There were lots of thoughts in his mind before Ranjit did what he wanted to do. He thought of using his approach to get rid of this case. He thought that may be after spending few years in jail, he would be a free man. *But I would never get what I wanted in life.* Life would never be the same and compared to it, there is a much better option, *death.*

With a loud sound, Ranjit's head fell apart and drops of blood were on the bare back of the girl who was awake after hearing the bullet being fired.

Human tendencies are sometimes difficult to understand. When we like somebody and something very good happens to that person we tend to feel jealous and when we don't like someone and something very bad happens to him, it does not really feel good. Ranjit's death was a moment of triumph for Abhi for he was now the only person who deserved the property so he virtually won the case and revenge for attack on Roshen was completed. But yet, he was feeling a kind of vacuum for Ranjit Yashwardhan was his last family member even though they were not on talking terms with each other and finishing the case would meant that Roshen would no longer stay there with Abhi. But before all that, it was a time for celebration and Abhi was not one of those people who used to miss fun because of being too worried about future.

After the news of Ranjit Yashwardhan's suicide broke, hearing was cancelled immediately and it rendered Abhi as the only deserving owner of the property so the case of the royal property was effectively over. Mike was most happy on hearing this news. For him, this was like some diamond, for which he was digging everywhere in the earth, somebody just gave him and left. Priya wanted to celebrate it in some restaurant but before she could convey it to everybody, boys were in a bar drinking in the middle of the day, *that's their trademark whether they celebrate or they are disappointed.*

"Wow, it feels like everything ended abruptly. Just two days back we were struggling with the case, Abhi was proved to be a punk in the court and now suddenly, there is no case. Abhi will get the royal property, Mike will now get so many cases and I will go back to my quest of searching a good job." Roshen said when he was sitting with Mike and

Abhi with whisky filled in his glass and vodka in Abhi and Mike's.

"I don't think so. It was Abhi's idea which lead to all this. But I am still surprise how you were so confident that this would work. Your plan of telling in newspapers that Bhupendra Singh was ready to tell the court against his master could have easily backfired. If we had to come in court without him, Inspector Ashwin could have been in deep trouble for lying to the press or we would be in trouble for not bringing him up there." Mike asked Abhi.

"I know that. But take a close look at the things. My uncle never talked to me about this property. I never cared for this property but he assumed that I am going to give a fight for this property and he tried to make me look as a bad person. Only if he had told me, I would have taken back my claim." Abhi said.

"What us your point?" Mike was listening intently to Abhi. Abhi was his hero after his idea worked great.

"Secondly, he tried to kill me even when he did not have my photo. And that's why Roshen end up facing those bullets instead of me." Abhi paused for a moment, looked at Roshen, smiled and continued, "All this proves that he was a man who always reacted before he was ready. I never knew that he would commit suicide but I was sure that he would certainly do something before the hearing. And that's exactly what happened, just little more than my expectation." Abhi smiled once again and took a sip of vodka from his glass. Roshen was now convinced that Abhi truly deserves to be a prince and have that '*Royal Property*'.

"So Roshen, what are your plans now?" Mike asked Roshen who was amazed by the fact that Roshen was jobless but still was staying with Abhi just to help him in this case. Sometimes he wondered if Roshen wanted to take advantage of Abhi but it seemed foolish to speak seeing how close friends they were.

"Don't know. Perhaps I will go home now. I have nothing left to do here. Plus now everyone in family expects me to live with them as long as I don't have a job."

"Why can't you just stay here? I will find you a job in two days. And if nothing comes, you can take care of my property. I will pay you for that." Abhi said as he was predetermined to make every effort to make Roshen stay with him.

"I don't think I can do that. It's very big property and working for you would fell icky." Roshen said.

"Icky? What are you saying dude. I will pay you more than you expect and I promise, I won't interfere in your working. If you want you can manage the orphanage. I need help to handle this property, after two days, I will start working as editor. Then I won't be having time to manage things and I would love if you are around to help me out." Abhi said in his trademark tone Roshen was already familiar with.

"Are you still going to take that job?" Mike interfered who was surprised to hear that.

"Of course I am. I promised Rohit. I will do that job until he finds a new editor, as long as it takes." Abhi said. Roshen knew that Abhi would do that. All the time that he spent with Abhi, made him think a little like Abhi, and he was feeling that too.

"Hmm, it's up to you now. What can I say?" Mike said as he surrendered in front of Abhi's decision, "I have to go now and listen to some dialogues my wife would say for drinking at this time of the day. I suggest you to go home as well, you are also married now. I bet you would get some words from Priya as well."

"It's okay; we will stay a little longer." Abhi said as Mike stood up to leave. He was now relieved and wanted to complete the conversation with Roshen which was disturbed last day with Mike's call.

After Mike was gone, Abhi and Roshen continued to chat for more than half an hour, though, this time, they were talking more than drinking and somehow there chat was looking like it would never end. They talked about everything from cricket to politics then about girls, they talked about the time when they were not talking to each other, Priya and then Abhi asked Roshen what happened to Kriti.

"Did you ever saw her again?" Abhi asked, they both were still sane but the thought of Kriti made Roshen a little sentimental.

"No, but I heard that she broke up with that guy as well. Yesterday someone called from office and was telling that she is not coming to office for last two days. I think it was a good thing that we are not together now." Roshen said in a low voice.

"I know this kind of girls. They just need to change boyfriends once a while."

"I think you were right when you called her a bitch. I just want to slap her once." Roshen said deep in his thoughts.

"There is no need to do that, that girl lost you, she slapped herself this way. I know you will find a better girl with whom you would love to marry."

"Are you kidding, I hate the idea of marriage. I love my life this way and will live this way." Roshen said acting like Abhi used to when they first met.

"You are an asshole" Said Abhi with a smile. He knew Roshen did not mean what he said and will get sentimental for the very next girl he would find. But he also knew that there was nothing wrong about it. *Life has to move forward.*

EPILOGUE

"Wake up now. Do you want to be late on the first day?"

Abhi heard Priya's voice as she was busy cleaning their room. Usually she did that before Abhi woke up but today, it was supposed to be Abhi's first day on his new job so he had to get up a lot earlier than his usual time. In the last two days, he had spent most of the time with Priya and Roshen. Last night, he was with Roshen drinking beer in his room and now when he tried to recall it, he just remembered sitting with Roshen. Before he left the bed, Priya gave him a cup of tea. *Being married is not bad, someone you love wakes you up at time and then gives you tea, awesome start of a day,* Abhi thought.

"Is Roshen still sleeping?" Abhi asked taking a sip of the tea which tasted great at the moment.

"Yeah, you guys were talking till late night."

"Hmm"

After about half an hour, Abhi was ready to go. It would have taken even less but Priya kept on disapproving everything he chose to wear, a thing Roshen used to do till now. *I have two wives now.* Roshen was still sleeping when Abhi left. It felt a little strange taking up a job when he had a big property waiting for him but Abhi knew, he had to do something and keeping his promise to take up that job would be the best thing to do.

"So, what will you do today?" Abhi asked Priya standing at the door of the apartment.

"Don't know. I will start with paintings soon. Or I can go to see mom also. But don't worry; I will be here when you will come back." Priya said with a smile as Abhi started walking slowly towards the lift. Priya waved to him and so did Abhi.

Abhi had a long day in the office. He was told how to do things for few hours and than was straightaway given some responsibilities which he did not expect on the first day. The work took longer than he imagined and by the end of the day, when he saw his wrist watch which Roshen had given him, it was seven in the evening. Surprisingly, he was so busy in his work that he did not realize office timings were over. Time passed very quickly and at the end of the day, Abhi felt he had done something. This job was not that much boring as he had thought. After his assignments for the first day were over, he headed back to the apartment.

On his way back, Abhi was wondering what Roshen and Priya would be doing at the apartment. Neither Abhi called them all day nor had he received any call from them. He stopped at a flower shop and took some for Priya, *another thing he was doing for the first time in his life.* After half an hour, he reached the apartment and found Priya waiting for him at the door. *Being married is great*; he thought the second time that day.

"Wow, you were waiting for me; so sweet of you." Abhi said as he kissed Priya on her cheek giving her the flowers.

"Thank you." Priya said looking at the flowers. Abhi went inside the apartment and moved towards Roshen's room. He was dying to tell Roshen how good his day was in the office exactly the way Roshen had done when he came back from his first day at the job. But this time, Abhi was going to tell this story to both Roshen and Priya together.

"Roshen, where are you?" Abhi shouted and opened Roshen's room but to his surprise, Roshen's room was empty and all his stuff was gone.

"Where is Roshen?" Abhi turned and asked Priya, half expecting the worse but perhaps he understood where he was.

"He is gone. I tried to stop him but he had made his decision." Priya said feeling that he let Abhi down by letting Roshen go.

"How can he...Why didn't you tell me?" Abhi was feeling worse than the thought of losing all his property made him ever feel. Words were hardly coming out of his mouth.

"He told me not to. He knew that you wouldn't let him go. I am sorry." Priya whispered.

Abhi did not know how to react. He knew that Roshen was thinking of going back, it was beyond Abhi's imagination that he would leave without telling him. He sat on the couch. He wanted to hit Roshen in his face and tell him, 'how dare you leave me' but only if Roshen was there that time.

"He gave this for you." Priya said handing Abhi a folded piece of paper. It was a letter handwritten on a white sheet on both sides.

Abhi looked at Priya for a moment and then at the letter. *Roshen should work on his handwriting,* Abhi thought as he started reading it. It said,

'Hey Abhi,

I know you are angry because I left without telling you. You have every right to go nuts for this but I know it would have been very difficult for both of us if I continued living with you. If you were in my place, you would have done the same.

I have written this letter because there were a few things I could never tell you. You would have made fun of me even if I somehow had tried to tell you all that. You are such a pain in the ass, you never listen to anybody.'

Abhi smiled. *So he wrote a letter to abuse me, jerk.*

'The day I first met you, you were a different person than you are now and I hope you know that even I was a different person. All the time I spent with you in this city, changed me. when I came in the city, I had everything I wanted all my life and now when I am leaving, I have nothing but an experience which will tell me how to live my life now onwards.

Abhi, you are a clear winner the way you lived your life. I think you were right when you said that life is not to survive, it is to live. I may have survived till now but now I am going to live it and I hope you will never change the way you always lived. Don't worry; I will soon get a job and may be a new girlfriend, but I will never forget what happened here in my first job and with my first girlfriend.

One more thing, I still think it was suspicious the way you were helpful to me since very first day. You helped me with money, in my relationship and most of all; you helped me by telling my father everything I could have never told. I confirmed from Priya that you are not gay but I still doubt you are a bi. Just kidding, you are a great friend.

Finally, one thing you are very bad at, that is taking care of your wife. Dude, you always told me how good you were whenever it was about girls and you can't take care of such a sweet girl whom you love so much, it really surprises me. Priya is a great girl and I want you not to be stupid and do whatever she wants; and that also in the positions she likes.... kidding again.

I wish you a happy life ahead. I will keep in touch....Bye.

P.S. - Don't come running behind me. I hate kids who do that.'